LAUREL

One Little Boy

"Here is a book for those who have the courage to look deep into their own hearts. It is the story of every adult who, like Kenneth, may be unhappy because he knows now what he fights and so, in a sense, gives up the fight, as Kenneth started to do. Because of the wisdom of his mother, he got the chance early in life to learn to do battle more courageously. Here, too, is what a therapist should be—warm, kindly, firm."

—*The New York Times Book Review*

"Should be recommended to doctors, to psychotherapists and those using their techniques, and to a wide though selective audience that would find its skillful projection of a professional point of view to a lay public of constructive value in better understanding the place modern therapy can take in helping those in need. A dangerous subject, in any other than highly trained hands, this book helps chart the way, provides a measuring stick."

—*Kirkus Reviews*

"An unusually good and moving record. *One Little Boy* will be appreciated not only by professional workers, but also by any parents who seek enlightenment in furthering as best they can the growth and welfare of their children."

—*U.S. Quarterly Book Review*

one
little
boy

DOROTHY W. BARUCH

A LAUREL BOOK
Published by
Dell Publishing Co., Inc.
1 Dag Hammarskjold Plaza
New York, New York 10017

Laurel ® TM 674623, Dell Publishing Co., Inc.

ISBN: 0-440-36631-3

Reprinted by arrangement with The Julian Press, a division
of Crown Publishers Inc.

Printed in the United States of America

There has been one previous Delta edition published,
November 1964.

First Laurel printing—August 1983

ACKNOWLEDGMENTS

The acknowledgments that come in connection with this book are somehow more intimate than most. They are born out of personal contacts and shaped with warm appreciation.

To Hyman Miller, my husband, I am grateful not only for the sharing of his broad medical knowledge and his very deep grasp of its psychosomatic aspects, but also for the long hours of going over the manuscript together; for the searching moments when, as a scholarly critic, he was perceptively challenging and for the cherished moments when, as a tender human being, he was deeply moved. Without his help this book could not have been written.

To Martin Grotjahn, Teaching Analyst, and Director of the Institute for Psychoanalytic Medicine of Southern California, I am grateful because out of the breadth of his background and the penetrating quality of his mind he gave so generously of his knowledge and time. I am grateful for the exquisite ability to identify which is his, and for the way he has of going into his own thoughts and bringing out the essence of what is needed to shed more light.

To Virginia Kirkus I am grateful not only because she is a great master-artist versed in technical judgments but also because she is gifted with a feeling for what people'are reaching and struggling after, and because she saw and conveyed so ably what was needed here and there to bring what I was saying into more expressive forms of communication.

My thanks go to Kenneth's father and mother for the courage they showed, and the vision beyond themselves, in letting their story be written and for going over and checking the manuscript. Nor are these my thanks alone. They are the thanks that I know will come from many fathers and mothers who read and gain deeper insight and understanding made possible only because of the willingness of Kenneth's father and mother to share the sad and hurtful and unglorious moments that most people must hide.

And last and most important, my thanks go to the real Kenneth. When I asked him if I could write the story about *him* to help other children, three years had gone by since I had been seeing him regularly. Earlier he had had two-and-a-half years of psychotherapy—play therapy at first, and later of more grown-up talk. Then for three subsequent years he had come in on his own initiative from time to time.

I explained to Kenneth that the secret things we had considered as inviolable confidence would become visible to whomever read the book. Even so, Kenneth said that I should go ahead. Somehow, now that he was different and bigger, the secrets of the past no longer seemed so important. From this I gathered that to him the secret things had become illumined with a sense of their rightful time and place in the world of reality. They meant comparatively little in the face of the new challenges and hopes that filled his life.

When Kenneth read the finished manuscript, he said, "I was such a sad-sack in the beginning. I felt sorry for me. I'm still me, but different. It's tremendous how I've progressed."

For this I am most grateful of all.

If, in spite of all these rich and generous contributions, errors have crept in, these are solely my own.

This book was written for those who want to know what children are like underneath the usually-spoken thoughts. It is about One Little Boy. It could be about any child.

In the twenty or more years in which I've worked with parents and children, I've never seen a child whose thoughts and feelings were not in one way or another basically like this one boy Kenneth's. Just as every child has eyes and nose and mouth similar in structure and function, so also does he have thoughts and feelings basically similar. Just as his eyes and nose and mouth are differently put together so that his face becomes uniquely his own, so also are his basic thoughts and feelings differently put together to make his personality and his problems uniquely his.

A child takes little and big things from the world about him and around these he weaves fantasies which are strange and primitive. A child may, for instance, sense his parents' unconscious feelings, as Kenneth did. Or a child may misinterpret his parents' feelings. He may imagine that he is more wronged, more threatened, less preferred than he actually is. In either case, the resentment and anxiety and fear and guilt which color his fantasies then grow out of proportion and problems emerge. Nonetheless, the elements that go into his fantasies are basically the same as those of any normal child.

All children's intimate thoughts about life and sex and love and hate are basically similar. They are strange thoughts to us who have come to believe only in logic. And yet it helps a child if we as parents or doctors or teachers can understand.

Kenneth's story is a true story. It is specifically about Kenneth, but it might be about any child. Naturally it has been disguised enough to hide the identity of the people it portrays. Nothing is attributed to Kenneth, however, that he did not say or do.

His parents were fine, intelligent people. As is true of many people of our time and turmoil, they had their own problems that dated back to their own childhood and disturbed their relations with their children, with each other and the happiness within themselves.

Because Kenneth was gifted beyond most children in shaping words beautifully to light up dark places, I chose him to write about as the One Little Boy to express things for many.

In one child the same basic thoughts and feelings may create disturbances that result in asthma or in school failure as with Kenneth. In another they may result in behavior or personality problems, in problems of discipline or in problems with other children. A third child, given more love and more understanding, can come through without any lasting hurt.

Feelings and thoughts are not absent because they are not spoken. *Not-heard* does not mean *not-present*. Even if your child does not have problems like Kenneth's, he can still have similar feelings and thoughts.

The thoughts and feelings of childhood are deep and dark. If they creep out inadvertently and we meet them with the shock of believing them abnormal, we do one kind of thing to a child. If we meet them with the embracing sympathy born of having already encountered and seen them as natural, we do another.

This book may bring the shock of encounter. But it may also establish an attitude of friendlier familiarity with a child's deeper thoughts and feelings. This is my hope. For then love and understanding will replace the condemnation that comes from not-knowing and will help other children grow more sturdy and secure.

ONE LITTLE BOY

To the real Kenneth who has given of his heart and mind so that some day, perhaps, through the spirit of what is told here, the children of the earth may achieve a measure of peace.

He knew from the beginning that his father and mother were having trouble. It came to him at night from their room across the hall.

"In bed they keep thinking dark thoughts."

He would lie rigid. His legs tight, his chest tight, his breathing tight in his body.

"They're apart and leading their own lives in the same house. Separate in one house. They speak to each other but they don't really talk. Each is to himself, ignoring the other. It makes me feel they're divided...

"It's frightening."

He wondered what the sounds meant coming from behind

their closed door. The strange night sounds. The formless hum of voices. Sounds as if his mother were sobbing.

He would try to sleep. He would try to break up his body's tightness by moving.

"I toss and turn and I can't go to sleep. I hear them in their bedroom. I want to hear and I don't want to hear. . . And when I fall asleep finally, my sleep is heavy with dreams.

"The real trouble is with their loving. That's where the real trouble is."

He could not voice this until much later; not until after he had been coming to me for psychotherapy for many long months. But he knew it and held it tightly inside him across from the threshold to words.

When his mother first came to talk with me about him, he was failing in school. The principal had said he would have to repeat the second grade.

"Won't it be bad for him?" His mother's hands, lighting her cigarette, were trembling. Her face, though, was without expression except for the politeness of her smile.

He'd been having difficulty in school for some time past. But she had not expected failure. Now that it had come she was at a loss.

"You see, I don't want to push him. If it's the best thing for him. . .well, I'll want him to stay back and repeat the grade, of course, and I won't try to protest it. I just thought it might be wise," with apologetic concern, "to see what a psychologist thinks.

"Ken's a perfectly normal boy. He's always been normal. He's a very good child. He doesn't have any particular problems. And I've always felt he was bright. More than average." Her dark eyes were serious. Her black hair, parted from the taut skin of her forehead, fell in unruffled waves to a knot at her neck.

"I can't understand his failing in school. His father's very intelligent. That's what first attracted me to him...He was top man at college, always at the head of his class. He did well, too, in his engineering courses and, although his job now is modest, he's well thought of by the engineering firm for whom he works."

She lit another cigarette. "I never got to college though I've always wished I had . . . I'm just a high school graduate. But last year . . ." she hesitated . . . "Well, last year I took some I.Q. tests myself . . .

"I was relieved and surprised when they came out high . . .

"You see . . . I've always felt I was a failure."

She looked away. Out through the open window to the sky, and I had the impression that this girl, who outwardly kept such tense control, was suffering deeply inside.

She turned back toward me and for a moment looked as if she were asking me to hear something she could not say.

Then the poised air took over once more. "Let's get back to Kenneth."

Systematically she laid out a picture. Ken had talked before he was a year old. He'd been a good baby. Clean. He still was clean. A timid child, not pushy. He never quarrelled, either with his brother, Brad, who was three years younger or with other boys on the block. She did worry sometimes because he had no friends. He didn't seem interested in other children. But, aside from the school problem, what had worried her most was his asthma. It had started when he was just under three, while she was carrying Brad.

"It's terrible to see a child almost strangling, gasping for breath almost every night."

Again her hand shook. Again the apologetic look. The doctor had said the asthma might be psychosomatic and had recently told her that Kenneth's slowness in school could be due to emotional difficulties. "Emotions are powerful," he had said. "They can bring about problems. They can cause failures. They can use potential ills that lie un-erupted inside the body to express in body language what the person cannot endure to express with his tongue."

Now that the school crisis had arisen, she thought it time for me to have Ken. Would I look him over? And if I thought he needed psychotherapy, she had already decided he should begin.

We arranged for her to bring Ken in. And meanwhile I was to call the school.

The principal talked with me. Ken was doing poor work. That was all. He could not be promoted. It wasn't that the child had been absent too much because of the asthma. It wasn't because he was lazy. Though he wasn't ambitious either. He seemed to try to do his work, but in a half-hearted way.

"But the main thing, I believe, is that he just isn't as bright as the average child in this particular part of the city. So he falls below the average and can't keep up. Most of our children, you see, come from better class homes and are brighter. As you no doubt know, his family lives right on the borderline between our school district and the neighboring district where the homes are smaller and the families aren't of such high caliber or income group. His I.Q. is a hundred and eight, whereas most of our I.Q.s are above a hundred and twenty.

6

So you see it's no wonder he can't keep up . . . I'd like to co-operate with the family. But I'm afraid we can't go against our policy. We can't promote a child who is below average. We've told him he might fail, hoping to spur him on a bit. But it didn't. Perhaps a transfer to the school in the neighboring district would be helpful. At least he'd be with children whose I.Q.s are more compatible with his . . ."

I hung up the phone drearily. When would school people see children as children and not as paper I.Q.s?

I also talked with the doctor. In his opinion, the asthma was psychosomatic. Just as another child might develop an eating problem, a sleep problem, temper tantrums, bedwetting or a dozen other behavior problems as outlet for emotional disturbances, so the child with an allergic constitution can develop asthma or hay fever, eczema and the like. However, it was not alone the things that happened to him that created the emotional problems. It was what a child imagined or made out of them in his own mind.

We planned time ahead when the doctor would give me a more detailed report.

Kenneth came in three days later.

He was a big boy for his age. Seven years and eight months. Sturdy in form and build but without the air of sturdiness. The droop of his shoulders belied sturdiness. Pale freckles. Pale hair, like cream colored petals dulled toward fading. His eyes were intelligent. Widely set. Perceiving, but as if trying to pull back from what they perceived. A hiding look in his eyes. A pulling back look about the whole boy.

His mother had explained to him that they were coming to me because of what had been happening at school; for one thing to see what might be done about the principal's suggestion that Ken repeat the second grade.

I told Ken now that I was a pretty good trouble-shooter and if I knew how he felt about it, I'd probably be able to help him. "The most important thing to me, Ken," I assured him, "is what *you* want to do. How you feel about it, yourself."

He looked at me and past me, out of the window. And then he answered, in a tone that lay between voice and whisper. Flat, without color or inflection. "It doesn't matter."

He sat on the couch next to his mother, and I saw that his breathing was tight.

The kind of straightforward talk, man-to-man as it were, or as between two grown-ups—it worked with some children. But it wasn't for Kenneth.

My mind ran ahead of the facts. I felt that this child was a hurt child. Something or many things had hurt him so much that he dared not voice his wishes. Or, what was even more probable, he dared not try to reach down to discover his wishes himself.

Right now, at this moment of our first meeting, the most important thing for Kenneth lay far from decisions about any school. The most important thing now for Kenneth was to feel that I was his friend. Not demanding in friendship. But steadily watchful. Feeling with him and accepting. Giving him sturdy warmth to count on without pushing him to give of himself in return.

TWO

"You can even call me Dorothy," I said to Kenneth. "But it doesn't matter. And I'm not the kind of doctor who gives vaccinations and such. I've got a playroom around the corner with clay and paints and puppets and lots of other things to play with. Let's go in there now."

He looked toward his mother. Neither seeking nor demanding. Neither quizzical nor protesting. He just looked.

"She'll wait here," I offered. And I held my hand out and led the way.

He did not take my hand.

I wondered: Would he accept friendliness from me? Would he be able to? How long would it be before he could discard

9

the un-childlike apathy and dare trust me even a little? How long would he remain folded back into himself?

He followed me down the hall without protest, and I kept my hand extended behind me. I thought of children much younger who, even while refusing a proffered hand, still found a minute measure of comfort in knowing that it was there to reach for and cling to should one wish.

We turned the corner and I opened the playroom door.

Brown floor. Good and hardy with its covering of linoleum tile. Green-blue walls that could be washed down. A sink with running water. A stool to sit on. Nothing more. Only a closet door half ajar giving promise of playthings to explore.

I wondered if he felt as I did the comfort of this small, bare room with its lean look of sparseness and space. No demanding clutter of things to be done with. A room where a child, strengthened by the therapist's support, could gain courage to explore what lay in his mind. A room where feelings that had towered inside him like overwhelming ogres could be whittled down to manageable size. Where fantasies that had brought dread and confusion could be looked at without too grave fear that their faces would turn real. Where wishes that had seemed too close to the border of terror could be transformed into shapes that might soundly approach promised lands. Where yearnings born in the lost years and now become hopeless might return to past seekings and move on with new hope. In this room, events that had been distorted by disappointment or by misapprehension, fear and fantasy could be depicted and dramatized. They could be given form so solid that a child might finally reach a place where imagination could still communicate with horizons beyond reality while effort and action remained compatibly geared in with the real world about.

Kenneth went with me into the playroom.

He looked toward the door of the closet that stood slightly ajar. But he said nothing.

I followed his look. "Perhaps you'd like to see what's in there?"

He stood wheezing.

He needed to find out that I was available to him as a therapist is always available to a patient; that I would be beside him steadily, helping him to explore into himself. This he could do through playing out his feelings, in the way that children reveal themselves, in contrast to adults who talk out what is inside. There would be no restriction on his bringing out the ugly, the absurd, the fearful. To this end he needed to discover that he could feel and say anything, and, for the most part, do what he wanted. I would try to tell him simply.

"This is a place where you can do just about anything you wish. You don't have to ask me."

He moved to the closet. Wheezing. Saying nothing.

When I opened the door he fingered the box with the doll-puppets in it. Still silent.

"Perhaps you'd like to see it?" I asked. "Shall I get it out?"

He shook his head slowly. And with voice held in and almost tearful, he said, "I'd rather not."

I thought his eyes moved to another box. "There are crayons in there. See?" I lifted it. "Would you like them?"

And again, pulling breath in, he whispered, "I'd rather not."

I realized then that to him my asking seemed like pushing. I was being too much like a teacher prodding him toward doing. Or like mother seeking accomplishment through him? Or like father?

I moved the stool over to where he stood and sat down beside him. Both of us silent.

He continued standing there in front of the toy closet, his shoulders slack, his arms at his sides. He kept on wheezing. I sat and he stood until finally he turned his head slowly, his body unturning, and he looked at me. Without wish or question. Without expression. Not staring. Merely looking.

I said very softly, "Some people would rather do nothing." He needed to find out that I would not push him.

He nodded almost imperceptibly and stood a while longer. Then he turned and moved to the window and looked out. Wheezing.

I moved my stool up quietly beside him and looked out with him. The two of us looked out together in silence. I, not intruding; just being there with him.

After a while my ear caught a sound. He had spoken scarcely above a whisper. One word—"Dorothy"—out into space.

Gently I put an arm about him to let him know more surely in the early body-language of a mother with her baby that I was with him. My arm around his shoulder could say it better and more convincingly than my tongue could.

He leaned toward me and looked at me piteously, as if he wished to cry and couldn't.

"Please, Dorothy, I don't want to do anything." He hadn't believed me. Almost tearful, but without tears coming, he went on, beseeching me not to force him. "Please don't make me."

A lump rose in my throat.

"No, dear, I shan't."

After another span of silence shared between us, I added, "This is a place where you can do what you want. You can do nothing if that's what you want. You don't have to live up to anything here. You don't have to be a big boy. You can be a baby, even, if you wish . . ." and very low, "you can play you're my baby, if you wish . . ."

He sighed and the tightness seemed suddenly to loosen a bit.

And then, for all his seven-year-old bigness, he climbed into my lap and curled up like a Great Dane puppy, knuckle-boned and gangly and yet almost soft in his helplessness.

Still saying nothing, he lay there. And I saw that he breathed a little more quietly until our allotted time was up.

THREE

When Kenneth had gone, one fact stood in front of me. He was a child so hungry for love that he wanted to slip back to the beginning of his life in order to make up for what he felt he had lacked. He wanted a second chance at being a baby so that he might gather into him the sense of being loved for himself, not for what he did or accomplished.

The next sessions with him bore this out. He came to the playroom each time and climbed straight into my lap. No dubiousness. No hesitance. This was what he wanted. Contact with me as though I were his mother. To be held by me quite simply. At first nothing more.

And then, he experimented further. He began whining

softly like a baby coming out of sleep into hunger. A small and plaintive but demanding whimper. I got the nursing bottle off the play shelf and filled it and he sucked, guzzling it as hungrily as if he had been pulling at it with toothless gums.

But there was still another thing he wanted. Cautiously he moved his hand to his face, his eyes warily on me. He was coming to life. And then he put his thumb into his mouth and sucked it. Sucked. And sucked. His eyes creased and a small twinkle came into them, like a message risen to the surface to tell me that underneath he was saying: I want to be your naughty baby and have you willing still to hold me. Not throw me off because I'm not good.

So I held him all the closer and let him suck.

Inside of myself I wondered: Why was he so starved? True, there existed in his mother the too heavy emphasis on accomplishments. But I felt this did not tell the whole story. There must be much more. What had his fantasies spun out of the thread of his experiences? Where did it come from and what did it mean, his deep hunger for love?

I had seen his mother again, shortly after his first time with me. She was curious to know what he had done.

I told her, as I tell most parents, and most children, and had also told Kenneth: What a child actually does in his therapy must be between him and me. Only then will he feel free to bring to me those things that he has secreted in little grubby hide-away holes in his mind or that he has interred more spoorlessly for fear that they will frighten or destroy.

"It's going to be tough on you," I told her. "Tough not to have reports of what happens in Ken's sessions. Difficult to trust me when you know I'll be keeping things from you. You'll no doubt want to scold me roundly at times and tell me you resent it. If you do, I can take it . . ." I laughed and she laughed, and the thin-drawn skin across her forehead seemed less taut.

"But I won't leave you in the dark. I'll be giving you my own appraisals of Ken, as this seems wise, and we'll talk over his needs and his progress as we go on . . ."

I told her also that I'd spoken briefly with the physician and had another longer conference scheduled, and that I would continue to work closely with him as I always do. I was already in accord with his opinion that the child's school problem was emotional. I reiterated that emotions can even affect intelligence test results by making it difficult for a child to put out or show what he really knows.

I told her, too, that I'd gone to the school in the neighboring district and had talked with the principal there, a young woman with a sureness about her and, at the same time, warmth. When I described to her what had happened to Kenneth in the other school, her eyes snapped with brisk indignation. "That makes me sick," she said, vigorously unpolitic. "The very idea of attaching intelligence levels to the kind of house one lives in. How about Abraham Lincoln and the log cabin in which he grew? And as for labeling a child too dumb to progress when he has an I.Q. of a hundred and eight! That's absurd. I don't care in the early grades anyway whether they're up with their class or not. I keep them with their own age group. That's much more important. It's too great a blow to a child to be left behind. You tell Kenneth's mother to bring him right on over. We won't demote him. And we'll see what can be done to make him as comfortable and happy as we can."

I had sung hallelujahs as I'd left her. Some of my enthusiasm for her and her school must now have communicated

16

itself to Ken's mother. We decided it would be best not to call on Ken to make the present decision. He wasn't really ready to. It was beyond him.

As Ken's mother was leaving that day, a curious thing happened. I commented that it might be a good idea for me to see Ken's father.

"Later on," she hesitated. And I felt the reluctance that lay behind her words.

When I went into conference with the doctor, he gave me a rounded and detailed report.

"I first saw Kenneth at about six years of age," he told me. "He was a malnourished child, very slender and exceptionally quiet in his behavior, even more than is usually the case with asthmatic children." He went on with various details. Among these was the fact that Kenneth had been burned on his arm when four and had had a tonsillectomy at six.

About the asthma he elaborated: "His asthma had been foretold, so to speak, by the eczema which he had in infancy and by a frightening episode the first time his mother gave him egg when he was about five months old. Although there had been no feeding difficulties prior to this, he immediately and violently vomited up the egg, his lips and tongue swelled, and hives appeared all over his body. He cried and acted just as though he were having an attack of colic.

"His pediatrician recognized the apparent allergy to egg and advised the mother to omit egg and all egg-containing food from his diet.

"As Kenneth grew, he was able to eat egg without any obvious ill effect. I held in mind, however, that his asthma might still be basically due to some sensitivity. It had started when he was just under three.

17

"There was another good reason for this and why his asthma could have been foretold. His mother had suffered from allergic hay fever for years and it is well recognized that the tendency to allergy is frequently inherited and comprises a constitutional factor that is almost universal in childhood asthma.

"It was no surprise, then, to find when Kenneth was skin tested that he gave very markedly positive reactions to many substances such as certain foods, pollens, cat hair and house dust. This confirmed what I had suspected, that Kenneth was constitutionally allergic.

"Experience has shown in many cases of childhood allergy that either avoiding exposure or being immunized to the substances which produce skin reactions will relieve or even cure such symptoms as eczema, hay fever and asthma. Kenneth's mother was therefore advised to remove all the reacting foods from his diet and to avoid exposure to any of the dust producing substances which gave skin reactions. In addition, Kenneth was given a series of injections to immunize him against pollens and other substances to which he was sensitive and which he could not avoid.

"Despite my shots and the mother's faithful and conscientious regimen for almost a year and a half, Kenneth continued to have more or less constant wheezing and sniffling with frequent severe attacks of asthma.

"Generally if there's no marked improvement within three or four months, experience has taught me to look elsewhere. With Kenneth I observed that he seldom spoke a word to me in spite of the fact that he came in to see me once or twice a week for more than a year. And he never complained that his injections hurt. He passively offered his arm over and over each time to be hurt again, and then hurried from the room as though not to be caught expressing his dislike of the pain and of the doctor who caused it.

"I've never seen Kenneth's father, but his mother's a very fine and intelligent girl. She's done everything in her power to help Kenneth. But somewhere, I've felt, there's been an emotional lack that I'm sure she hasn't been able to control; some emotional immaturity somewhere in her, just as in most of us. She's taken Kenneth to numbers of doctors and has obviously tried to hold in her apprehension over him. And yet just as obviously she's made it apparent, as though she were saying, 'See, I'm not complaining, but I don't think you can help Kenneth, and if you can't I'll have him as a burden for the rest of my life. It's up to you to do something about it.'

"Other indications from things that were said and things that were not said made me feel that much of Kenneth's asthma might be due to emotions which made use of the allergic tendency with which Kenneth had been born.

"People born with an allergic tendency can give positive skin reactions to many substances and yet have *no* allergic symptoms. In some the symptoms never develop. In others the symptoms may be set off by exposure to whatever they are allergic, or by an infection or by fatigue. But in many when such symptoms appear, it is also a sign that some emotional difficulty is using the allergy as its outlet.

"I mentioned earlier that Ken is unconsciously using his asthma as a way of working out his emotional difficulty, much as another child might use a stutter, persistent vomiting or what not. However, Kenneth's use of his allergy is a faulty way of solving the emotional problem. So is another child's lying or whining or poor eating. No matter what the final problem is, the child needs help in discovering less faulty ways of handling the emotional pressure inside him.

"Meanwhile the eczema or hay fever or asthma is just as painful to the patient when it is set off by emotions as when it is brought on by foods or pollens or infection or fatigue. It is the same illness and causes the same suffering. It is just as much beyond the control of the sufferer. And the sufferer has just as much right to relief. As long as the illness is induced by feelings that remain unconscious, they are as invisible as unknown germs. When you bring them into focus and into Kenneth's field of vision, then *he* will be able to control *them* instead of their controlling him.

"To Kenneth's mother I had repeatedly suggested that Kenneth's asthma did have this emotional component and I referred her to you quite a while back. She hesitated, however, because of the expense and time involved. And also, no doubt, because like a good many parents, she failed to realize that a child's need for psychotherapy does not mark him as abnormal any more than does his need for 'shots.' It's just another kind of treatment to help a psychosomatic condition or a behavior problem to get well.

"I'm sorry Ken has had to fail in school. But I'm glad at least that this has finally furnished the necessary incentive to bring him in."

Kenneth's mother's next appointment came after Ken had been playing out his need to be a baby. She arrived looking tired.

What was disturbing her, I wondered. And did it have to do with Kenneth's starved and hungry search for acceptance and love?

She jumped at once into a report on having enrolled Ken at the new school. He seemed content enough, she said, with the shift. At least he'd made no comments. She herself liked

the principal and the teacher seemed friendly. But . . . Well
. . . Did I really think Ken would be all right? Was he really
bright? Had I been truthful with her in saying he wasn't
dumb? Could emotions actually interfere with school per-
formance?

She stopped suddenly and sat frozen. Like a man I'd once
seen side-swiped by a car, sitting on the curb, motionless, torn
between disbelief that he'd been struck and a terrified urgency
to spring up and fight. And then came the question that I'd
known from the beginning would inevitably come.

*What could have caused Ken to become so emotionally
disturbed?*" The question rose out of silence and hung over
a precipice of silence when it ended.

Presently she dug into her bag for a cigarette. And again
I noticed the trembling of her hand.

"Really, I've done everything I could for the children. I
didn't nurse Ken. I guess I should have, though the doctor
told me it's only good if you feel like it, and for some reason,
I didn't. I know now, too, I tried too hard to break him of
sucking his thumb. All those devices, you know, to make him
stop, which he did except sometimes at night in his sleep."

She was using an almost servile politeness as if through
obeisant pleading to ward off some danger.

She puffed for a few moments in silence, her hand continuing to shake.

"Maybe I wanted Ken to be too good. But then, he has been
a good child. Always. I've always been proud of him. I was
when he talked and walked early and was good about toilet
training and about giving up his bottle.

"I've tried to give him and Brad everything I could. The
best care. The best doctors . . ." She crushed the cigarette stub

21

almost brutally in the ash tray. "Vic—he's my husband. He says I spoil them."

And then, all at once, she put her hands over her face, her nails white with the pressure of her fingers digging into the bone of high cheek and forehead. "Oh, I know it. I know it. It's all my fault. I'm no good for Kenneth. I should never have had any children. I've known it all the time. I know I'm ruining them. I didn't really want them. Vic didn't either. Only, my mother thought I should have them and I listened and persuaded Vic to. I don't know why I did it. I'm too self-centered. I guess they feel I push them aside."

She stopped as suddenly as she had begun. She lit another cigarette, drawing the smoke in hard as if trying to pull herself together through sheer physical effort. She was struggling as I'd seen many mothers struggle, and particularly the mothers of allergic children, torn between wanting to want a child and somehow being held back.

"Don't you think instead of sending him to this new public school I should send him away to boarding school? Wouldn't that be much better for him?" Her tone was insistent.

I asked her to tell me more about how she felt.

"I know I'm really not right for them. I should never have had children. I'm not mature enough, not wise enough." She spoke now as though she were reciting a memorized passage, apologetic that its lines were not fine enough. "I'm too serious. I can't be the kind of mother children like. I'm not carefree and gay. They would have been luckier if I hadn't had them . . . I worry over them too much. I'm afraid I won't do well enough by them. I'm not good enough. Something might happen to them. An accident. They might get hurt."

She went on to tell how at the beginning of World War II she had been afraid they might be injured in enemy bombings. And so, when Ken was four and Brad a year old she had sent them away to live with her mother and father "in Peoria where it was safer." They'd been away for a year and then had been brought back by her parents, who had settled near her brother's home here.

"I often think if they'd stayed away I'd have felt better . . ." She stopped, suddenly frozen. "It sounds as if I didn't love the children at all . . .

"Do I love them?" She sat staring. "Do I?" as if trying to drag something out.

"I was afraid to have them."

She said it in a flat voice without intonation. When she was a child, her mother had told her horror tales about pregnancy. And about giving birth. A woman's body invaded. Torn apart. A woman's life over. After a woman had a child, she had no further chance to accomplish anything. Her mother's life had been over when she had had her, Cathy. Cathy's younger brother wasn't the cause of misery. He had somehow brought solace. It was Cathy, the first child, who had put an end to all living . . .

"My mother never called me pet names. Never 'dear' even . . ." The shell around her voice broke and the tears came.

Later she spoke of her father. He'd been a changeable and violent man. Playful at times—on such moments, to Cathy, the sun had burst from behind fog. "The day would suddenly be filled with color, not gray." But, as suddenly, he would pull away, grow angry. Yell at her. Beat her with his belt. "Once he gave me a little toy elephant. I mislaid it. I went to my mother and asked if she'd seen it. 'Run along, Cathy. I'm busy. Don't you see?' " And so she had gone to her father. He looked at her, sombre. And then an ugly swear word slapped out at her through his lips.

"How could I have been so careless?" she sobbed. "Don't you see? I've never been any good."

She talked until she ran out of words and, it seemed, out of tears.

I told her that in every child's life things happen that make trouble, not alone because of their having occurred but because of what a child makes of them with his mind's spinning. What he conjures up out of them, what they mean to him. What he imagines and fantasies—these count as much as the actual happenings. Even when everything in the child's life seems all right, the fantasies he himself creates can frighten and disturb him. So also may the feelings by which he keeps the fantasies hidden but alive inside him. . . . All such things enter in. They had with Ken. They had with her. Her life mattered as much as Ken's. Her feelings mattered.

"Can I talk about me? About myself to you? You mean you're not too busy? You want to hear about *me?*"

I nodded, seeing as surely as I'd seen with Kenneth: Here was another child who was hungry for love.

A reservoir without water cannot take water to those who are thirsty. Neither can a starved person feed another out of full bounty. Cathy needed a good mother to become a good mother herself.

FOUR

Kenneth came in for his next session wheezing. But this time, instead of climbing into my lap, he stood haltingly in front of the open door of the cupboard containing the play materials. For several long minutes he stood. And then he began tentatively to finger the various boxes that lay open on the shelves with their contents exposed.

I sat very still, knowing how important a moment this was. He had dared move away from the shelter of my arms. He was like a baby taking his first exploratory steps alone. What would he do now? Would he crawl back again to be held? Would he turn to me to choose something for him out of the cupboard? Or would he be able to choose on his own, prompted by his own impulse and volition?

He was very quiet and so was I.

Presently, he reached in slowly with both hands. I watched, not stirring except for the soft gliding of my pencil taking notes.

On Kenneth's part now there was no pause for further deliberation. No wavering from one box to another. Before his reaching hands, his mind had already decided which box he would have.

In the split second of his reaching, my mind went forward with him. What he chose would bring its own message out of his unspoken thoughts. The choice of itself could communicate some of what lay in his mind.

My pencil stopped suddenly when I saw what it was. For this restrained child had chosen out of all things the most unrestrained. This good child had sought out of all things that which portended least good. He had chosen the box of soldiers armed for bloodshed with bayonets and machine guns and cannons. The reaching hands had betrayed the fact that behind his mild, expressionless face, he was holding thoughts that had to do with hostility and fighting and war.

"These are the enemies and these are the Americans." He spoke in a whisper, his breathing tight, his wheezing audible. Out of another box he chose two small airplanes, "one for the enemy and one for us," a blue "get-away car" and some paper bags which he blew up and made into "hills for the soldiers to hide behind."

Arranging the brown paper hillocks at opposite ends of the room, he placed the enemy soldiers behind them at one end, the American soldiers behind them at the other end.

"The soldiers," he said, "they're all hiding. But it won't do you any good. I'll get you. Chzzzrrr, chzzzrrr, here come the shots!"

He was energized, swooping from one end of the room to the other, carrying imaginary bullets in his hand back and forth in swift-curving arcs. His voice still was only a whisper but with the opening of fire his breathing was freer and his wheezing was less.

Strangely, though, there was no explosive gunburst. No crash of cannons. Only occasional anticipatory streaks of sound like bullets whirring through the air. Premonitory sounds of things to come. Building for the attack. Skirmishing. But not ever attacking.

Until his whisper again crept out from behind the screen of wordlessness, I could only wait to learn of the happenings that in his mind's visioning were accompanying the bullets' flight. When he spoke again, I had to strain to hear.

"That one hid. And that one. But I'll get you. I'll get you . . ." clenching jaws tight. "I'll kill you yet . . ." But he couldn't. His face showed disappointment and dismay. "Oh, dear, that one's hiding. And that one's hiding. And that one's using the get-away car. He's trying to escape. . ."

Then, with fresh onslaught, addressing the enemy, "It won't save you, you'll see . . . Up goes my plane. MMMrrrrr . . . mmmmmmrrrrr . . . Here come the bombs. Ahahah, that got the tire. That got the fender. That ruined the gas tank. That broke the steering wheel. I'll get rid of the car for good."

But again his face fell. "Oh, dear! That soldier jumped out. He ran and hid . . ."

He was an American flying against the enemy. He was on the winning side. He was bitterly intent on killing. But he could not kill.

Always something happened. Men ran to cover. Men hid.

27

The bullets and the bombs hit objects, not people. An enemy plane was bombed to bits. Enemy houses were demolished, mountains laid bare. But never the people. The people always got away.

Once he came close. "I *think* I got one. No, he went running. There goes another. This one comes out and surrenders. He's a prisoner now. And the next one, I'll get you this time you . . ." But the vindictive whisper dwindled into a wheeze. "No, he escaped too."

Piteously whining, Kenneth came and pushed himself close against my side. "Won't you tell me, Dorothy, why do they always escape?"

The next time was the same. Until near the end. After having opened fire in anticipation of wiping out an entire company, he had once again made them all run to cover. But now he came to a sudden halt. Very slowly he dragged his feet over to where I sat, and he stood there, not close up against me, but about a foot away, wheezing, an imploring look on his face. And then, with an intake of breath that was almost a sob, but still tearless, he put a new question to me. It came out astonishingly simple and brief in its overwhelming necessity. "Dorothy, am I a nice boy?"

"Yes, Ken," I answered, "I think you're a very nice boy." And he slid into my arms.

The question that followed was as tight as a handkerchief wadded into a knot. "Then, can I do it?"

I knew there was only one answer, spoken encouragingly, "Show me about it." For he had to bring into focus whatever it was he wanted to do. Instead of using words to confess it, he would, in the way of childhood, shape his confession in play. But my answer contained more than its words. It contained my eagerness to have him share any and all feelings with me. It contained, also, my inner conviction that should the action-pathways that carried the flow of feelings become too dangerous or frightening, I'd be there to help him stop or divert the flow into safer paths.

That my certainty gave him more certainty was evident. He went into bombings anew. But this time his voice rose above the whispered, checked fury. "I'm going to kill you." It came out clear and glad.

Swinging his arm like a scythe in a wide-circling swathe, he cut across the enemy troops, knocking them over. The mouth noises changed. They were no longer the hum of things anticipated. They were the sharp cracking explosions from a machine gun belt. The jubilation. "This man killed them. *I* killed them all . . ."

It was then I noticed that his wheezing had stopped.

But only for a very few minutes. Then the cringing caught up with him once more. "This man, he didn't get them all. They're coming after him, the ones that are left. Put him in the get-away car . . ."

His voice dropped again to a whisper and the breathing grew tighter. "I knew what would happen," with a kind of despair. "I'm knocked in the head, but I still can steer. What'll I do? I'll have to hide . . ."

Out of the get-away car he lifted the soldier, himself, whom he'd called alternately "this man." He shoved him desperately into one of the paper bags. "He tries to hide in the cave here. But they come and find him . . ." He groans. "They got him. They got him in the leg . . ."

And then came a theme that was to be repeated time after time through many long months, a whispered prophecy of things to come and already imagined. "This man was shot in the leg. Right in the knee. They have to cut off his foot. He'll have to have crutches to help him walk."

Ken lifts the man out tenderly, groaning in low agony, propelling him in limping hesitation across the floor to "the hospital" where I sit.

With face blank and solidified, he lets go and the soldier falls on his back on the floor. Ken sits, arms limp, head bent forward, eyes straight ahead, expressionless. A dry, thin whisper creeps sibilant through the rising wheeze. "This man. They have to cut his foot off. He's hurt for good."

It was only after the session was over that I remembered a dream his mother had told me the day before: She had seen a foot, without a leg. An amputated foot. "As if it were cut off."

Feet nauseated her. She remembered: her father's feet. "Smelly, and heavy with sweat . . . Feet were feet of clay. She thought of mortality. Life was so vulnerable. It could be cut off so easily, like a naked foot.

FIVE

At home Kenneth wheezed steadily for the four days and nights between that session and the next. He was quiet. He was good. But he coughed and struggled for air during the night and breathed with painful tightness during the day. The doctor did what he could.

But Kenneth kept on wheezing.

The doctor questioned me: Were we moving too fast? I said I'd watch it; perhaps we were. Kenneth had been such a good boy for so long that it was frightening him to open up to his own view this other part of himself—a part that lies deep in every one of us—hidden but ready to splash out in the bitter word, in the twisted temper or in the flood-burst of mass riot, lynchings and war. In small or large measure we manage, each in our own way, to keep it underground, according to the smallness or largeness of the hurts we have suffered, according to the onus we have leveled at ourselves for unwelcome feelings and according to the quantity and depth of the bitter gall we have stored.

Kenneth had been hurt. I knew only part of it all at the moment. Anger had, as result, accumulated inside him, and had given rise to fantasies mixed with tremendous fear and guilt. He could not show this anger or he might do too much. He might lose the last remnants of his mother's love. Therefore, unconsciously he did let the anger turn back on its course till he himself was both donor and recipient in the pain of illness, in the tragedy of failure, and in the fantasied hurts more dreaded than that of the wounded soldier and more dreadful to bear.

He would have to bring anger to the surface where he could look at it and with my help gradually understand and integrate it into the portrait that he painted of himself in his mind.

Release had to come as a primary step if he was to survive in wholeness. I knew this. But I knew also that if it came too fast, it would threaten to inundate him so that he might close up the floodgates anew with reinforced blockades.

In his next session, Kenneth again chose the soldiers. At the start, he dared not follow his impulse to strike down the enemy. Hesitance encased him like lead-gray fog. But at last his desire broke through—throwing a spotlight on terrain that had been veiled from view. And with it, his face was illuminated.

His bombs struck not only mountains but men. His bullets, born in swift flight by his hand from enemy to enemy, crackled mercilessly. Faster and faster. The open voice replaced the closed whisper. Free breath in and out of lungs replaced the stoppered sibilance of his wheeze.

"The bomb got em!" jubilantly. "One man. Two. Three . . ." He went down on one knee, crouching in triumph over the strewn men, his yellow head bent to inspect the havoc he had finally managed to deal after such struggle. His words spilled out. And with them, in the risen excitement, a small trickle of saliva dribbled from his mouth to the floor.

He looked at the dark spot of spittle on the linoleum in stunned silence.

"I—I'll clean it up," he whispered.

Stiffly he rose from his bombs and his soldiers. He walked to the closet hook where a cloth hung and to the sink where he wet it. He wrung out the cloth like a well-taught robot, and brought it back to the spot on the floor.

"I—I didn't mean to get the floor messy."

"I know it, Ken. But really, in here it doesn't matter. You can do lots of things in here that you think aren't proper outside."

But he could not hear me or dared not show that he'd heard.

Slowly and with painstaking thoroughness he mopped the wet space, went back to the sink, washed the cloth out, wrung it, mechanically hung it back on the hook. And without another word but with the rasp of his wheezes breaking the silence, he came straight into my lap.

I thought: To him messing means being bad. So also do injuring and killing, even in play, mean being bad. They're different sides of the same coin, different facets of resentment, or anger, or hostility—call it what one will. Inside of Ken, the reservoir was full to spilling over. In his play, when it was draining out through the drama of killing, it did not need for the moment to drain out in asthma. In such play, though, it showed more of its true form. Ken could not escape its meaning as completely as he could when it came out in sickness or failure. Sickness and failure were great camouflagers. With them he could say in the space beyond words where unrecognized thoughts exist more as feelings: I'm being good, not naughty. I can't help it, after all, if I fail or am sick.

Since messing was less bad than injuring or killing and since injury and killing had frightened him so much, it was obviously not the messy spittle in itself that had sent Ken back in fear to being a baby seeking arms' shelter. The spittle was merely the proverbial last straw.

I would try to help Kenneth get firmly acquainted with the milder forms in which his "badness" showed itself before tackling what to him seemed more dangerous. I would arrange materials and set up the playroom so that it would automatically limit what Kenneth brought out. Instead of waiting for him to get the soldiers from the cupboard, I would have clay or paints out on the floor in readiness, as an invitation to mess rather than injure or kill.

Then bit by bit as he tackled what was less frightening to him and saw that he could live through it without being overpowered by his feelings or deserted by me, he might perhaps gain courage to explore more deeply. I would try as we went along to help him feel less guilty and less afraid and to understand his feelings better, not through mere words of explanation but through the experiences which we would share. Perhaps then—very gradually—the more dreaded feelings might lessen until he could say, in effect, I can handle what's left of them. I'm not really so bad! I don't need to be afraid any longer that my feelings will push me into such terrible actions that I'll either be deserted or destroyed. I needn't turn them back on myself and punish myself with illness and failure. I needn't keep them walled off and hidden as if I were telling myself, "These feelings, they're *not* part of *me*." Instead, I'll be able to let them slip into place as part of what I am. If he could reach this point, he would no longer need to stand over himself, cruelly denying himself and trying to relish denial in place of pleasure. He would no longer have to drain energy from his school work, for instance, in order to keep reinforcing the walls. The energy that had been used for hiding would be freed for work and play, for enjoyment and laughter, for friendship and love.

All this I hoped might eventually happen. I would try to help Kenneth achieve it. But essentially it was Kenneth himself who had to do it. Would he be able to? Was there sufficient courage and vigorous urge left in him, not only for living but for aliveness? How far would Kenneth be able to go?

I had finger paints waiting ready for him next time, right in the middle of the floor.

"What are they? . . . Where are the brushes? . . . Where are pictures to color? . . . I don't do well in free art in school. I like paint-books better. I almost never go outside of the line."

Poor, tight little Kenneth, afraid of what his brush's unsteadiness might mean, feeling that he must not go beyond the line—seeking the shelter of its neat constraint.

I told him you did this kind of painting with your hands, that was why it was called "finger painting."

He wanted gray. And when we got a blob of it onto the paper, he touched it very gingerly with one finger. "Look how dirty my finger got."

He stared unhappily at it.

"Will my finger get clean again? Will the mess come off?"

"Let's try with the soap and water at the sink."

We did. And he saw.

He took a big breath. "It does come off."

He started afresh. With the tips of all the fingers on one hand. With whole fingers down. With palm in, slithering, until the sticky paint was covering the inside of his hand. "See how dirty?"

Again doubt. "Will *this much* come off?"

Back to the sink. "I'd better see."

He scrubbed until I wondered if he'd left any skin.

To the paints with both hands sliding in. Back to the sink. Again to the paints. Again to the sink. Paint and scrub. Prove that he wouldn't have to keep tell-tale signs of dirt on him, then he could get dirty. But the proof was hard to believe. And so it had to be sought again and again until he could finally say with more certainty, "I *can* get them clean."

Both hands went in, then, and the paint slid up past the wrists. "I'll make them real, real dirty." He was smearing the paint now, over the backs of his hands and between his fingers. "I'll get them all dirty. Ahhrrr, ahhhrrrr, I'm messy! Ahhrrrr!" He growled and stuck up his hands toward my face in a menacing gesture as if he were going to smear me. A pouncing gesture, his fingers spread like claws. His head was back, his eyes guardedly on me, and a sound came from his lips. It was laughter but it was not the full-throated sound that rises from the gay heart. Rather the ghost-sound of an echoed, hollow denial of fear.

I wondered if he saw me swallow.

Even though it was thin and shallow, coming from no farther back it seemed than his palate, still this was the first time in the short long month he'd been with me that I'd heard Kenneth laugh.

SIX

I wondered what Kenneth would do in his next sessions. Would he be able to move on? Or would he retreat? There was no predicting.

Because of his great hunger for love and acceptance, he was like many other people I'd seen, adults as well as children. They open up quickly, seeking warmth, seeking to show themselves and to know that warmth can continue. They want desperately to trust, and they do, momentarily. Helplessly they put themselves, physically or figuratively depending on age, into another person's lap. It's as if they were saying: Here am I, defenseless and weak. Take care of me, please. But they dare not stay open and trusting. They feel too guilty in their demandingness and the guilt gets in the way of loving. They feel too afraid of wanting to avenge themselves against those who inevitably fail to give them as much as they wish. They tighten up. They retreat. This was especially true of asthmatics I'd worked with. But it was true also of others whose love-hunger was deep.

What would happen with Ken?

He had at least seen that not only could he be dirty bad; he had seen that he could be menacingly bad. He had followed his impulse to attack. In his fashion he had threatened me, perhaps attacked me in fantasy. I didn't know. But in reality he had let go of himself safely, albeit for an instant only. And this time he had accompanied the letting-go with control rather than with retreat. He had pounced and had stopped himself before he had actually attacked me. He had shown himself that he wanted to be bad and that he wanted to direct his badness against me. He had shown himself also that he could let go and stop without actually harming me or losing my acceptance. He had seen, too, that nothing had happened to him. I had been strong enough to look at his expression of hostility with him and had neither punished nor deserted him for it. He knew this now. Not through anyone's saying it to him, but through having lived through it himself. He could now be a fraction less afraid of two things: of his own inner feelings running wildly out of hand, and of retribution from me. The guilt and fear aroused by his feelings could in consequence be a little less keen-edged.

As if to tell us we were on the right track, there had been a brief let up of the asthma after the last session. But I warned myself not to assume too much. There was only one way to know. To wait and listen and watch. Meanwhile, however, I could not help wondering whether Kenneth would maintain some of the feeling he had gained momentarily in the last session? Would he dare go on opening up? Or, when he came in next time, would he be knotted in tightness once more, daring only to whisper and wheeze?

He came in smiling shyly and reached for my hand and held onto it as we walked into the playroom. I felt as though he were telling me we had shared a secret. This was good.

He was timid at first but he gained in courage. And the next few sessions were full of play with paints and wet clay. Messy play. Freer play, breathing more freely. He ceased running to the sink to wash up. He revelled instead in the clay and paints covering his hands. He slithered it through the chinks between his fingers. Patted it; got it under his nails and over his wrists.

He did not make any move to attack me again, nor did he show in any way that he remembered having done so. But the meaning of his messing was clear. "I'm bad. I'm dirty . . ."

I said, "You like to be bad and dirty," smiling at him.

He didn't answer, but I knew from his small smile that he'd heard.

One day a curious thing happened. He was unscrewing the tops of the paint jars and got a bit of red on his fingers. I thought I saw him shudder. I wasn't sure. But he went at once to the sink and washed. And by now this was an unwonted act.

The episode of the red paint threw him back for a bit into more gingerly attack. But again he gathered courage. Each time he smeared more vigorously, not caring to depict anything, merely wishing to smear. He alternated with clay which he watered down till it grew quite "gooshy." And he liked particularly the gray and brown paints.

Brown brought its own special kind of freeing. Brown was

to smile about secretively. Brown was to giggle about in the silly way of a small boy hiding a grubby worm in his pocket. Brown was to sniff about slyly. Brown was to grin about as shamefacedly as a virgin listening to a salacious jokester between puffs of his after-dinner cigar.

"Well . . ." Ken finally brought it out. Brown was like "big job."

So we looked, knowing together. And gray became like "big job" too. Dirty. Bad. But fun.

But brown was not without danger. Nor was gray. Neither paint nor clay. They were all right in their place, to be regarded lightly or seriously according to mood. Gray bits of clay dropped into a bucket of water could be whirled around and "flushed down the toilet." Brown paint could be spattered and slithered over sheet after sheet of paper. Clay and paint mixed together into a pasty dark mush could be squeezed in the hand and dropped in gobs through the opening between palm and little finger into water-filled bowls.

But paint and dirty clay could be frightening too. They could reach into widening destruction. Paint, for instance, could lead into tortuous lanes with hazardous endings.

"Look, it can be twisty," with forefinger streaking a white snake-line across a gray-brown, pasty sheet. "It's a house. It's twisting along the paper. It's a strike of lightning. It's hitting the house. Whammm. Pfffirff. The house fell in . . ."

We were back again where we'd left off with the soldiers after having made a wide detour from death-dealing blows. Under my breath I think I must have uttered some word of hope: If only in the time spent on the detour he had gathered enough courage and strength!

There was a slight tightening of his breath. It always told me when he was approaching danger or trying to avoid dan-

41

ger's threat. It was a sure sign of a frightened attempt to block off what was imminent. As sure as the blind mole's hillock evidencing that some little scuttling thing is alive and hiding in the ground underneath, too frightened to come out and fight. Some children show they are blocking or burrowing under by wriggling silliness, by giggling evasiveness, by hesitance, by stutter, by aimless, tangential acts. Adults show it by tension in face or body, by the prolonged silence or the rush into inconsequentials . . . Kenneth always showed it by the tightened breathing and often by the drop of voice and the rising rasp of a wheeze. All of these brought evidence now that he was blocking off a dreaded impulse, as before he let his soldiers kill.

"The lightning's hitting the house," he repeated. "And the people . . ." Pause. Silence. Tightness. And in a whisper, "The people escaped. The whole family . . ."

This is even closer to the truth, I thought, than the destruction of those soldiers. But I could not guess the exact meaning. I still had to wait.

Clay could also lead into danger and retreat.

One day he was fashioning it freely into "pieces of big job." Sitting tailor-wise on the floor, he lifted these high above his head and let them drop, one after another. "He-ha!" sung low. "He-ha, he ha!" easily. "Now what'll I do with you?" addressing the clay chunks. "I'll make you bigger. Into a bomb. Ow-wow! Ow-wow!" He dropped it repeatedly.

"Now I'll make a pointed end. Both ends pointed. I'll make both ends noses. It's a different bomb this time. Bigger. *A father bomb!* I'm going to throw you down on your nose . . ."

But he could not go through with it. He stopped.

There rose again the sibilant signal of danger . . . The wish and the blocking. His breath was blocked inside him as was

42

his desire. It could not come out any more freely than could his impulse. All that could come was the wheeze.

I made a note in my mind: A father bomb which he was bent on destroying. And the danger too grave.

SEVEN

His asthma that night was bad again.

For a while he returned to unformed messing in his sessions, leaving all targets out of the picture. But this, I soon saw, was a kind of retreat in which he might pick up reinforcements and gather strength. For as suddenly as the retreat had come, so came the next attack.

Again I was the target.

He had been building a "mountain" of clay, adding pieces bit by bit, almost painstakingly smoothing over the mound so that each accretion became an intrinsic part. "Smooth it, smooth it," he sang softly. "Bigger and bigger!" Until a great, fertile mountain bulged under his hands.

"Spank it. Spank it!" repeatedly, somewhat louder.

"He, he, he! I'm spanking it. I'm slapping it. I'm banging it. Ahhhrrrr!"

All at once, with sudden energy, he lifted the entire mound of clay from the floor and, springing to his feet, stood with his arms high over his head. A great blond giant holding the enormous weight of that great bulging mountain high in the sky. Higher than Atlas holding the world.

Just as suddenly, he hurled it down on the floor. He almost fell forward in the violence of his throwing.

He straightened up. And in his eyes was a gleam of ill-wishing as wicked as any I'd seen.

"There, you . . ." he ground his teeth at me . . . "You . . . You . . . *I hurt your ears.*"

In his triumphant freedom his voice was angry and his breathing clear. He lifted the mountain above his head again. He slammed it down. Lifted it. Slammed it.

A victorious and venomous laugh broke through. "I hurt your ears."

He came a step closer and peered at me. Flatness was coming back into him. Almost imperceptibly the high-lit moment was dimming.

I listened for the tell-tale tightening of his breath and wondered if it was my imagination that his shoulders seemed slacker.

"Your ears are hurt?" The words unmistakably dropped toward tonelessness instead of rising. Quite unmistakably they carried the uncertainty of questioning that which had been certain a few seconds before.

How could I keep this thing from happening? How could I help him know that victory did not have to droop like a faded flag? How help him feel that here and now, at this moment between us, there was nothing to be afraid of? That whatever was in him did not really have to hurt either of us, but that nonetheless the wish was strong and powerful and tangible and must not be denied.

I thought back on his gay pulsing triumph of a few minutes earlier. And, recapturing it, I laughed.

"You were feeling real mean and you *wanted* to hurt me!" I must have sounded as venomous and triumphant as he had. Though I knew and he knew he'd not really harmed me.

His shoulders went back and his head went up.

"Your ears *are* hurt." Not a question this time but an assured statement.

And then he said a curious thing that I was to recall many times later. There was a kind of longing in the way he said it, as if he wished that what he said were untrue. "They're not noses, your ears."

I answered the unspoken wish evidenced by his tone. "No. But you wish my ears did stick out like noses."

"Uhuh!" he nodded. And he smiled. "I did hurt your ears." The demon's gleam was back in his eyes.

I breathed a sigh of relief.

If Kenneth continued to block off and deny his anger it would remain distorted; it would grow and continue to distort him. Not seeing his anger, he would never learn how to channel or control it any more than a man can drive or control a car he cannot see. But as it emerged from invisibility into a visible reality, then he would be able to steer it into more appropriate paths and control it instead of its controlling him.

There is no child alive who is not at times angry at his parents. Too often we lose sight of the fact that honest loving comes side by side with honesty of feeling of every sort. Hate does not exclude love unless it is so tightly packed inside a person that it walls love up with fear and guilt.

A baby is born with hungers that must be nourished, not just fed. Only he himself knows when he has his fill. His emotional hungers may be too large for his parents to satisfy. They too have been children and often have not been satisfied themselves.

A child needs love and understanding. He needs chances to achieve according to his age. He needs appreciation for what he is and for what he does with his muscles and his mind. He needs to enjoy his body through its five senses without being made to feel that his body is bad.

When such basic hungers go undernourished, he grows angry. Then, unless he learns to express the anger forthrightly, and yet in unhurtful actions, he grows angrier. He also grows more demanding—obnoxious, cunning, sweetly charming or pathetic—but demanding no less. In one way or another he clings to immaturity as if this were a ticket that might eventually admit him to acts he has missed.

In his home, if from the very beginning a child is granted the right to let his anger show, in harmless ventings, each small squall is soon blown away to the winds. As he grows he can learn readily that there are some ways in which he may discharge such feelings and other ways in which he may not. But if anger is held under, it is not blown away. It is blown up by the child's inner fantasies. He imagines that his parents are more depriving than they are. He grows voracious in his inner hunger and guilty both for his greed and for his hostility. He imagines himself worse than he is, and must curb and control and punish himself in place of exerting constructive control. The whole matter becomes so painful that he relegates it to his unconscious and uses a disproportionate amount of energy in keeping it there.

Because of her own love-hunger, Cathy had not been able to nourish Kenneth's love-hunger. From what he felt of this he had spun his own imagined versions. He had grown inordinately hostile and had blocked this out.

As the doctor had indicated, his asthma was similar to another child's refusal to eat, or another child's shyness or constipation or lies. All such problems are ways through which children faultily seek to solve their conflicts. They all bring irritation or hurt to others as well as to the child himself.

In adult life, cupidity, selfishness, insensitivity may take the place of childhood problems. The list could be lengthened ad infinitum. Nor is the anger involved always vented in ugly form. Under the gentle cloak of martyrdom many a woman has made her husband's life miserable. Under the unselfish guise of working day and night for his family, many a man has brought loneliness to his wife. Under the banner of loyalty, democracy has stumbled. In the name of patriotism, massed phalanxes of youth heiled Hitler and let slaughter flow over the land.

When anger lies unadmitted, people often fail to differentiate fantasied wrongs from the real wrongs they receive. Not identifying the real wrong, they fail to expend anger where it is justifiably called for, and they grow angry mistakenly where there is no actual justification of cause. They let out on substitute targets years later the resentments that generated in childhood. Had they been able to bring it out, uncringingly, showing anger *harmlessly* to those who generated it, they would need no substitute targets, as Kenneth needed me now.

After all, Ken did not want to hurt me as me. I was only a straw-man, albeit a useful and necessary one during his therapy. I was the scapegoat on whom he could pin the effigy imaged in his mind of whomever he wanted most truly to hurt. Through me, if he went on with sufficient courage, persisting, he might finally discover less hurtful action-pathways along which to bring his feelings out.

The step he had just taken was a giant's stride for him, as great in reality as the triumph he had felt in his lifted arms holding aloft the mountain of clay. But he had to go further. Through having used me as substitute and found it undangerous, perhaps he could.

At least, for the moment, things were good. He was back on the floor. Pounding vigorously. Still full of energy. Still unafraid.

"I'm making bombs now," glancing up at me.

I nodded. And he went back to shaping the clay.

That night he had no asthma. But the next night he did. Fear had caught up with him once more.

When he came in next he was still in the grip of it. And yet he had an eagerness about him too. Dulled, not keen-edged, but palpable, nonetheless. As if, in spite of the fear, he wanted to get at something.

"Will you help me?" he asked, leading me by the hand into the playroom, not, as ordinarily, following me in.

Very apparently he had something definite in mind.

"Of course I'll help. Tell me what you want me to do."

"Help me make people."

We fashioned them out of clay, roughly and swiftly. "Four," he said. "A family. The father. The mother. The boy. The brother."

"Now bombs," he said, and he started making them intently.

I slipped back onto the stool and he went on independently.

49

He made a stack of bombs as roughly and swiftly as we'd made the people. Scooping up a fistful, he rose to his feet above the family, gazing down at them.

He stood. He paused. Poised on the edge of hesitation.

Then he flung his first bomb.

He flung the next. A whole barrage. "I'll get the father!" But his bombs went wide of the mark. "The mother!" But again his bombs went wide.

He aimed at the smaller boy. "Ahhrrr, I got him. I got the brother."

He swooped down for another handful. "I'll hit Brad some more. There I got him, the brother. I hit him good!

"Now the father. There, that got him. Now the mother. It got her too."

He surveyed the havoc and whispered, "That's enough." He'd kept the bigger boy intact. But he could not leave it so.

He reached for another handful of bombs and silently and grimly he finished him off.

Three things I'd noticed. He'd tried first to get the father. Then the mother. He'd missed both, although he'd hit the little brother without any difficulty. The trouble was not in his aim or in his ability to make his mark. As with his school work, the trouble lay in his emotions. His emotions wouldn't let him make it. But bombing the brother helped him dip into some sort of inner resource and he went back more sturdily to the bigger people and did more what he wished.

I noticed also his healthy wish to leave the older boy safe. This he had evidenced when he had whispered, "That's enough." But in spite of the wish to survive, he had still compulsively needed to destroy the figure representing himself. Why was this so?

The third thing told me why. His tongue had made one of those unconscious slips that betray what the person himself is not even aware of. He had called the little brother by his own brother's name. "Brad." This showed that the family was his family even though he himself was not able at this point to admit it frankly. He had, in fact, guarded it carefully from his own awareness by his meticulous adherence to calling the clay figures *the* father, *the* mother, *the* boy, *the* brother; not *my* father, *my* mother, *myself*, *my* brother. He had shown through his slip, however, that his play concerned not just any family but his own.

This then was why he had had to destroy the big boy. Himself. He had to punish himself, for one thing, because of his wish to destroy his family or someone in it. He had to turn hostility back again like a boomerang. He still could not let himself even imagine his anger's target and let himself live.

He could not yet admit consciously to himself that this was *his* family. He could not yet let his conscious mind know what his unconscious mind prompted, like the proverbial left hand not letting the right hand know what it does. This often happens. A person reveals what is in him long before he is ready to see it himself. The important thing with Ken for the present was that he had dared bring out his anger. He had dared disengage a little of it from the hard hidden nugget within to which he had previously kept it so well cemented. He had not averted it in a terrified curve away from its real target. He was coming closer. He had bombed not soldiers this time. But a family instead.

In the two months he had been with me, Kenneth had come a long distance from the cringing whisper and the complete blocking.

He had no asthma that night. Nor the next. Nor the next.

One thing in particular I wondered: What were Kenneth's own hidden reasons for going after his father? I knew some of why he wanted to bomb his mother, and there were plenty of theoretical possibilities as to why he wanted to bomb his father. But only Kenneth himself could reveal his own unique set of reasons.

In the face of his mother's reluctance, I had not pressed seeing his father. I did not know even what manner of man he was.

EIGHT

Recently Cathy had taken a giant step of her own. Something had transpired between her and her mother which Kenneth had witnessed. It no doubt had played its part in helping him open up.

In her own way, Cathy was moving forward. She had been coming to see me twice a week and was also coming once a week to a group psychotherapy session in which her doctor and I were joint therapists. "It seems I've been going at snail's pace," she said. And again, "It takes courage, this business of talking about yourself."

She had courage and she kept mustering it in her struggle to be honest about her own feelings. "You seem so much prettier when you fool yourself. It's not pleasant to look in the mirror or to look at unpleasant things that need to be looked at. I see now that I've always tried to look the other way . . . Keep things pleasant. Be a good girl, Cathy!"

By now she had given me a picture of herself as a child. Brown eyed. Slight of frame as now. Brown braids neatly tied with bows at the ends. A good child, trying to cajole her mother into loving her through the gift of goodness. "Please, mother, don't scold me. I didn't mean to break that pitcher. I'll be more careful next time." . . . "I didn't mean to bother you, mother. I'm sorry. My hand's not really badly cut. I'll go and put the iodine on for myself." . . . "Yes, I'll take care of Buzzie for you . . ." even though she was shuddering at the prospect inside. He was so big and unmanageable, her younger brother. "Being three years older hadn't given me enough of a head start to impress him with my proficiency. He was a demon as soon as I took over and mother's back was turned. But no matter what he did, I was always to blame . . ."

About her marriage and Vic she remained vague. I pointed out that everyday things, here and now, were as important as the past. That, in fact, the past of itself didn't matter except as it made its imprint on the present—both in terms of its happenings and the fantasies born then. We couldn't change the past. Our only point in understanding it was so that it would not continue to push into the present and future in ways that blemished the full colors of life.

When I said I wondered why she never mentioned her marriage, she said, looking hard at the wall opposite her, "There's nothing to talk about."

Life between herself and Vic was smooth and uneventful. "He's considerate and sweet . . . And as for sex," she volunteered, "I know that's important. It's all right, I think." There was a note of appeasement in her voice, as if by bringing me this offering she were waylaying further inquiry, like a good little girl saying to mother, "See how much I've done. Now you won't have to ask me to do any more."

I remarked on this to her and we laughed.

"There's really nothing more to tell," she rallied. "Vic and I have never had a cross word. Not since we've known each other. No quarreling ever. We never fight . . ."

But then, she had never fought. Not even as a child, except with Buzz . . . She'd been terrible with him. . . . The horror of what she remembered invaded her. She pressed her fingers against the tight, thin skin of her forehead over her eyes. "I don't like to see it. I don't like to look at it. I thought I'd forgotten it, blotted it out. . . ."

She remembered with frightening vividness how, when her mother had left her alone in charge of her brother, she had been unable to control him. "He'd get wild and loud. He'd yell at me with his face contorted. Like my father . . . I knew if I let him have his way, he'd get into mother's sewing or into the cookies she baked for dinner, and then I'd get beaten when she got home . . .

"Once, one awful day, I hit him. I was so wild with help-lessness, I threw him down on the floor. I sat on him and pummelled him. I banged his head against the floor-boards. I think now I wanted to kill him. I was seething with fury. I, too, was being like my father. Worse than my brother ever had been. Thank God I saw in time what I was doing. I stopped and got up and pushed him into the other room and locked the door to protect him from me . . .

"I've kept watch over myself, but I've known ever since. I have to keep those feelings under. If I let them out even for a moment, they might get the best of me. . . . God knows what

I might do to the boys . . . What I wanted to do . . . once . . . to Ken . . ."

She rushed headlong into what she had to tell me. She had to tell me. She had to shrive herself of it. In spite of the pain of it, she had to show it starkly in all its ugliness, not trying to soften it with any excusing of self.

"I told you I thought I should never have had children. I was afraid to have them. Not only afraid of the physical pain. But of not being able to control them, or myself.

"I've never seen the connection before, not until this moment. I was afraid of the Buzz thing happening all over. Each time I was pregnant I hoped and I prayed that my own children wouldn't be boys . . .

"As my pregnancy with Kenneth advanced I thought I got over those feelings. I was afraid, yes. I felt as if my body had been invaded and were no longer my own. I felt trapped. But by the end, I thought I wanted him . . .

"He was such a sweet baby. Good. Placid. No trouble at all. And then I let my mother convince me again. It was time, she said, to have another. And I felt she was right, that it would be selfish to bring up an only child.

"I went through nine months of hell. Even inanimate objects became possessed of the devil, and I struggled helplessly with cooking utensils and vacuum cleaner and washing machine until I wept bitter tears. And Kenneth, who had been such an angel, suddenly was into everything, exploring, investigating, getting into my sewing, into the cookie jar . . . I couldn't take it. I was afraid of what I might do.

"And so I put him into another room. And I locked the door.

"So help me. I left him in there in spite of his calling to me that he'd be good and begging me to let him come out. I

56

had to. I had to protect him against myself. . . . I couldn't take him when that kicking fiendish thing was inside me, possessing my body, twisting my entrails . . ."

Suddenly the pieces fell into place. *When Cathy was pregnant, Ken was just under three. Just under three, he'd developed his asthma.*

"Vic was patient," Cathy went on. "He couldn't have been sweeter. Out loud I was appreciative. But underneath I blamed him. Or rather, I blamed his maleness. It had gotten me pregnant. I wanted to pull that big thing off him. Never have anything more to do with it.

"And Kenneth kept on asking, 'Will it be a baby brother?' until I thought I'd go mad. And one day I screamed at him, 'No! No! No! Not another boy!'

"But it was. After thirty-some hours of labor, I groped up through the fog of ether to the realization that I had another boy . . . Another boy like Buzz. . . .

"Even now, when Ken or Brad come over for me to hug them, I'm afraid to. I might hug too hard . . ."

She was to return to the story again and again, adding more details, trying to throw them away from herself as though they were ugly, poisonous lizards. She could not understand why she had been so ruled by her mother, even to following her mother's suggestion that she have children.

"If I did what she wanted, perhaps she'd love me. But she still keeps on criticizing. Why do I handle the children the way I do? Why don't I make their clothes? The flowers I fix are too stiff. There is dust on the window sills. I don't defrost the ice-box often enough . . .

"I have to be good.

"Once when I was a little girl, I remember her saying,

'Now Cathy. You have to be good when you're here. And here too. And here!' Until I turned and asked in childish desperation, 'But where's there a place that I can be bad in once in a while?'

"Why do I always do what she says? Why do I take so much from her? It's childish. I can see now. I have to grow up. I can see I've made her my husband instead of Vic. I've turned to her, leaned on her, been dependent on her. It's about time I depend on Vic. . . ."

When she came in next, she told about having for the first time in her life—as far as she could remember—protested against her mother's criticism. Her mother had been provoked at her for going to a psychologist. Her mother had pressured, "Why go to an outsider? Why not continue to confide in me?"

Cathy countered, vehemently for her, "It's about time I stopped doing that, Mother. I'm a big girl now, don't you see?"

Kenneth had heard. Her small burst of anger, no doubt, had given his anger the green light, had sanctioned his bringing his feelings out. Without Cathy's progressing, we might have had to wait much longer for Kenneth to take his giant's step.

To me, Cathy murmured, "I've done it now. I've cut the umbilical cord. I'm a little frightened, I think. I'll have to learn to depend on Vic now." . . . And then her voice dropped very low. And scarce above a whisper I heard her question, "But can I?" And then she stopped and said no more.

NINE

Kenneth had dared unlock enough of his angry feelings to himself and to me for us both to see that his mind was on bombings of families more importantly than on the bombings of soldiers. Since no hurt had resulted, he dared move on to other things which he'd held clamped inside.

Again he wanted me to help him make a clay family. But this time the crudely shaped, visageless figures would not suffice.

"They have no parts." He found them lacking.

"You want to make them have parts."

He nodded. "You make them."

"O.K., and you tell me. You be the boss and I'll be—?"

"The workman."

He was obviously pleased with this arrangement. He picked out the big boy in the family to begin on.

"Make his ears!"

I started to make one ear and he voluntarily joined me, starting on the other.

"Now his eyes." He drew them. "And his mouth." He twisted the lead of my pencil into the clay to make the mouth hole.

"Now his nose," he directed. "You do that!"

I did.

"And now that thing," more hesitantly, pointing to where he wanted it.

I made it.

He smiled. "It's a big one. Like a big nose."

That sufficed. He needed no more parts on the big boy for the present. He turned to the father. "His has to be bigger!" with a shade of regret in his voice.

"Now the mother. Those two things."

So I made them.

And finally for the littler boy. "Don't make his big at all."

When it was done, he said, "Thank you," his politeness sounding strangely incongruous. I took it to mean my dismissal, as it apparently was. For, once I was up off the floor and back on the stool, he took over. The stage was set now. The act was his.

A strange and macabre act it was!

"I'll hide my daddy behind the mountain. . . ." He erected a mound of clay. "There, the father's hidden, but not enough." Again there had been the unconscious slip: "My daddy."

Then the quick covering with impersonality: "The father," again.

"The father has to be hid better than that," with anxious slowing of voice.

He looked around, and brought a towel out of the cupboard. He put it over the father and stood up. "That hides him real good," in a whisper.

He stooped and picked up the mountain of clay and gritting his teeth, he muttered, "Bombs away!"

This was serious business. He was down on the floor, leaning over the father, lifting the towel. "Yes, that hit him. I mashed him. His head. I mashed it." Yet, somehow his voice betrayed that his head was not all that he'd wanted to hit. His next words confirmed this. "No, it's this thing here I have to get."

He put back the towel, measuring with his finger the spot that he wanted to hit.

"I've got to get it. I've got to. I've got to mash it. Bombs away!"

He missed once, but not again. Compulsively he had to get it. Then he had to throw the bomb and get it again and again, marking the place each time with his finger on the towel that masked the demolition from view. But each time he lifted the towel and saw. "It's getting mashed. Now I have to mash it some more." At last his voice came louder, "Now, he's mashed all flat. I mashed it. Now his legs. Now his arms. I don't need the towel over him any more."

He moved on to the mother. Just as he had gotten rid of the father's male organ, so he got rid of the mother's breasts. And the little brother's organ and the big boy's, too. As if he were saying, "No protuberances allowed."

Suddenly, a clouded look of puzzlement came over his face.

61

He stood scowling as if he were trying to figure a difficult mathematical problem. He squatted. Picked up a hunk of clay. Made a rounded mound, surveyed it, as if this mound were in some way connected with what he was trying to solve in his mind. And then, slowly and distinctly, he stated what was bothering him.

"Where does his wee-wee come from?" he asked.

The protrusion gone, from where was he to perform this physiological act?

Then, still figuring but with the air of working toward solution, he picked up a pencil and drew a furrow along the top of the mound. He widened the furrow with his finger, and finally made a hole with the pencil in the furrow.

"There," he murmured, as if he were reaching the answer, "This has a wee-wee hole too."

The furrow and the hole were in the rounded form. The important function could still be performed. He was trying to persuade himself in his fantasies that the protuberance was not needed. A hole alone could take its place. His sigh and his smile showed that somehow this brought strange relief.

And then another thing about holes began to come clear. "They feel good." . . . "It feels good to them!" . . . "Things go in. Things come out. It feels good to the holes." . . . "And," smiling to me confidingly, "it feels funny to them where things go in."

"Do things go into your holes, too?"

He sat back on his haunches and thought.

"Uhuh," he nodded. "A thermometer. In my big job hole. And when I was little, a bottle in my mouth."

"That felt good?"

"Uhuh."

"The bottle?"

"Uhuh."

"And the thermometer?"

"Yes. And things coming out do too."

And so, holes served another important function of life. They brought pleasure.

Soon he began to show me more clearly that the pleasure of holes was also pleasure which he gave to himself.

There was the humming kind of pleasure, nearing sleep.

He made a clay child one day, and stuck his thumb in the child's mouth, a gesture reminiscent of the time he had sucked on my lap. Meanwhile he hummed softly with eyes half shut, until with sudden transition he announced, grinning, "He's naughty."

"But he seems to enjoy it," I answered, grinning back.

"Uhuh, but he shouldn't. He's bad." And he tore the child up. Many days, however, he came back to mouth pleasure, sucking or blowing bubbles like a baby through his lips.

Then, too, there was a rocking kind of pleasure, more orgiastic and wild.

Again with clay: "I'm making a mouse hole. A real dark mouse hole. The mouse goes into it . . . In goes the mouse." He poked in his finger. "Slidety slide. Slishy, slish," he chanted softly. "Squash, squish; slidety slide! Squash, squish, slidety slide," then louder, over and over, again and again. He dug in his finger and rocked back and forth, mesmerized in the motion, seemingly losing himself.

It was not until much later that he told me in words that he found pleasure in putting his finger in his rectum and masturbating in this fashion. But apparently already now he wanted, in his way, to show me about it.

That children universally enjoy their "holes" is a well-known fact. They get pleasure through sensations in their mouths and rectums. But a boy Kenneth's age usually enjoys his penis more than his holes.

But probably far more important than the pleasure he gave himself was the hope he may have harbored inside that were he to have only holes, his mother might accept him more. She had, in fact, accepted his holes. She had put a bottle in one hole; a thermometer in another hole. With these kinds of attention to his holes, she had given him her care. She had given him some of that which he most deeply craved.

Furthermore, in the dim past just before he was three when she was pregnant with Brad and Ken had asked, "Will it be a baby brother?" she had let him know she didn't want boys.

And then she had shut him out of her sight. She had put him off into a room by himself. She wanted a girl, not a boy. Perhaps he had sensed these things at that time and was remembering them now. Perhaps he was feeling that she would have loved him better had he been a girl.

This was not clear. It was clear, however, that for the present he feared to let the phallic symbol of maleness enter into the picture which his mind's eye made of himself. He showed this again vividly as he went out one day. He had, as usual, been playing with clay and some of it got on his shoe.

"Clean it up. Clean it up." He came to me, whimpering like a baby. "Don't leave it on my foot. It sticks out too far."

TEN

As Kenneth played out his fear of acknowledging his maleness, the wall that was holding back the acknowledgment started to show small wavering cracks. Miniscule. But enough so that tiny wafts of what lay behind seeped through.

He made clay worms. Snakes. Guns. But always something had to happen to them. He blocked up the wall again and pushed back the wish to own up to having what every male must possess. Worms could not remain worms; nor snakes, snakes; nor guns, guns. The shape apparently was too telling. He had to turn them into eggs or cookies or cakes; boats, canoes, what not . . . Inevitably he would put cracks or holes or hollows in these from which water would drip or splash.

One day he made a long thin cylindrical form, pointed at one end, a round knob of clay at the other end.

"It's a bomb with a ball kind of thing at the end," he stated.

Then, daring more, he ventured in his mind to transform it with a revision quicker than the blinking of an eye.

"No. It's a wee-wee-er—a penis—with that ball kind of thing," pointing down at himself.

But this was obviously too much. "No, it's not. It's . . . it's . . . it's a long nose with somebody's head at the end."

Again in his fantasy he was likening a nose to a phallus as he had the first time he'd asked to make body parts on the clay figures. And so a nose also was too dangerous a protuberance. "Grnnnhhh! I'll poke you in the nose, you. Now you've got only a mouth."

On another day, he surveyed a gun he had made. "It can work, too!" proudly.

But again this was too dangerous. He flattened the gun and called it a cradle.

"See," he said, "it's got wee-wee in it, the baby's cradle has."

He sat on the floor, pensively surveying the cradle.

"When I was at my Gram's house back in Peoria," he started recounting, referring to the time his mother had sent him to his grandmother for the year when he was four, "I dreamed one night I had to do a wee-wee. I was in bed and I dreamed I had to do it. And when I woke up I'd done the wee-wee in bed. I was wet . . ."

Noticing the glint in his eyes, I said, "You liked that."

"Uhuh," he nodded. "Only she said it wasn't good. Do you know, though? Grams didn't mind Brad wetting his bed in Peoria.

"Maybe," wistfully, "maybe Mother didn't mind when I

was a baby. But when you get bigger..." He broke off and, picking up a fistful of clay pieces, he sprang into standing and threw them, aiming soundly at a bigger chunk on the floor. In his mutterings I made out that he was hurling bombs.

It was then that he made another one of those telling unconscious slips.

"Boom," he said. "Boom, I'm bombing Grams. Soon there'll be nothing left of her. . . .Boom. Bombs falling. Boom on *my mother*!" And, quite unaware of the slip, "There now, my Grams is all gone."

On another day it was a snake he was making. He often made snakes and destroyed them. This time it was "a big one," he announced, very pleased.

Almost at once, he was crestfallen. "But my mother doesn't like snakes."

As he smashed it flat my mind clicked to another moment, not far past, when his mother had told me of a recurrent dream she had of killing snakes. In it she had come across one on a bare rock at sundown, and another sliding out from tall grasses. She had tried to step on them to destroy them.

Snakes made her think of her brother. He was a snake in the grass. When she was small, she had felt like stepping on him and on that small snake-like thing of his... She had smiled half-apologetically. That was like stepping on snakes in the dream and, she had continued, like wanting to destroy that big snake-thing of Vic's during her pregnancy.

I wondered if Cathy might inadvertently perhaps have alluded to some of these things in front of Kenneth. Or if he had possibly sensed her feelings from the way she had handled him in those earlier years when a child is so sensitive to the tensing of muscles and the tightening or unsmoothing of movement. A mother often unwittingly betrays through hands or shoulders or face how she feels about him and his body.

On still another day he wanted a clay child. We started to make one together and when the bulk of it was fashioned, I left him to put on the finishing touches.

He pondered a moment. And then he pulled a bit of clay forward from the base of the child's belly in a small but distinct protuberance, and getting the miniature dollhouse toilet from the cupboard, he had the boy stand up in front of it as if urinating.

Suddenly he was angry at the boy. "No, you don't, you. You sit down." His voice changed to wheedling. "Go now, do your duty. Do lots and lots for me." But, with annoyance returning, "Don't you stand up and wee-wee. If you do, I'll, I'll. . ." and he hit the boy with his fist, "I'll teach you. Smack. Smack. Smack. You're bad."

In his mind the act of urinating as a boy was bad. For he picked up the boy and spanked him into flatness and welded him roughly into the shape of an egg. "Put a crack in it," he said, "with a hole. It's a wee-wee hole. No," with firm decision, "it's not. It's a big job hole in the crack in the back. . ."

And addressing the amorphous figure directly, "Now you can do it. Make big jobs come out. *Like brown penises*!"

He laughed jubilantly. He laughed in triumph. "*Brown big job penises*. You can make lots and lots."

This was one way of solving his wish for maleness. He could have a brown penis, undangerously. If one got smashed he could make another. He could say to himself, as it were: You can still disregard that front protuberance that gets you in trouble. You can remain satisfied with something of similar shape that can stick out in back!

Again I remembered something his mother had told me, "When I was pregnant, Ken reverted to wetting his bed. I'd read that lots of children did this when they knew another baby was on the way. I'd stand and grit my teeth and shake with rage. I'd try desperately to remember the child training books saying that I must not show any anger or even notice the fact that he'd wet. To me, though, it meant another hour's drudgery, another drain on the little strength I felt I had left. I covered and dissembled and finally resorted to my usual defense during that awful period. I locked him away in his room..."

She had also told me, in contrast, that the bowel training had gone easily. "I just praised him a lot and he went along with it without any trouble at all."

The enigma was clearer. Kenneth had tried with worms, guns, snakes, to have a penis that mother would accept as Grams had accepted Brad's—wetting and all. Mother had scolded Ken for wetting. In his mind he had then imagined that the function of urinating, in order to be acceptable to her, had to be performed without a protuberance. Therefore the gun he made had to be turned into a cradle. All obvious projections had to be eliminated. Even noses were too suggestive to exist. Fortunately, though, there could be "brown penises" hidden in his body as substitutes for the missing part. Mother had praised him for his bowel movements. So this was all right.

When he finished that day, he asked if he could take some clay home to his mother, and he went out carrying a chunk of it in his hand as if it were something precious.

I thought of another boy, half as old, who had scooped

up handfuls of clay shaped into what he called "doodoos" and had, beamingly, handed these to me. "Here, honey," he had crooned, "look at the lovely things I made for you."

I wondered if Kenneth, now, was carrying the clay chunk to his mother to fashion into what he had called "a big job penis" to give to her as a gift?

Penises and bombs and big jobs—all one for the moment. I hoped they would not stay all one; that Ken would be able to separate them eventually. For the gift of love brought by a man to a woman is too often thought of as dirty, consciously or unconsciously, by many adults.

ELEVEN

All during this period Kenneth was bringing out his hostility more openly. With the continuing release and our handling of it, the asthma had dwindled. There had been no attack for the past month.

He bombed clay families. He bombed his Gram's and Gramp's house in Peoria and "the house where they live now, too." His play grew more and more messy. "Boy, what a time the mother has cleaning up!"

He saw a comic movie and told about it, his eyes lit with the demon of relishing the mischief in it, just as if he himself had committed the mischievous acts. "I saw Judy Jones. And they got fooled. They ate wedding cake and it was made out of soap and what do you think? Bubbles came out of their mouths..."

And what seemed best of all to him: "You know what happened yesterday? Brad fell in the fishpond. And he drowned... Well, almost."

"You kind of wish he had."

"Uhuh," grinning.

Nor was the hostility confined to his play sessions. I had warned Cathy about this. I'd told her that Kenneth's biggest problem was holding in his feelings. That if he were to grow up continuing in this pattern, he would not be the whole, intelligent and useful person he should be. That holding in hostility often also meant holding in love. That you can't be an all around holding-in person and then, presto, at a moment's notice generate and give out warmth.

She had smiled and had said, "It's like when you get married. All your life you've been taught to keep the stopper on sex feelings. And then all of a sudden, because you've acquired the ring and the license and the preacher's blessings, you're supposed to be free. I wasn't. I don't know if I am yet. But," once again hesitant, "what about Ken?"

I'd warned her that when Ken started coming out with his hostile feelings, he might splash them around home more than would be quite comfortable for her. That's what children usually do. The pendulum swings too far, temporarily, until the hostility diminishes to manageable size and they gradually learn when and where and how to get feelings out. That there is a time and place for everything and that there must be restrictions.

"You can't let him scalp Brad or make mincemeat out of him. You can't let him really hurt him. But you can help him channel his feelings into good healthy wranglings and fisticuffs right out in the open. Or, if these get on your nerves too much, you can at least let Ken know that you know how he feels. You used to be angry at your brother. Ken gets angry at his. You used to be resentful of your mother. Ken gets resentful of you. When he shows it, if you say quite simply, 'I know how you feel!' that in itself helps. Then, if you add, honestly, 'But it gets on my nerves when the two of you fight. So stop it,' he will know that you expect him to control his actions. At the same time, by seeing that you know how he feels, he will be less afraid to own up to his feelings. He will not have to go on hiding them as much."

She had nodded. And she had done it.

When Ken gathered courage enough at home to go after Brad, teasingly, with a dripping washcloth, threatening to throw it at him, Cathy had said, "I know you want to go after Brad. But not in the house. I'm not going to have the place soaked. If you want to have a water fight, run out into the yard."

She had reported this to me and had contrasted it with what she would have done earlier. "I'd have felt crushed. I'd have felt I was a no-good mother to have my two children fighting with each other. But I see now I'd have been pasting onto myself the feelings I used to have about my mother's being no good."

Kenneth's hostile bursts at home were still very mild and directed against his brother. And so Cathy managed to handle them without excessive anxiety. She might not have been able to if he'd gone overboard as some children do, or if he had shown more direct hostility to her.

But there was another kind of feeling that Kenneth was beginning to express to her that Cathy couldn't take.

She came in one day very depressed.

73

"I feel stuck. Trapped. Brad's been in bed all week with a cold. The walls are coming in on me. Maybe it's because I'm menstruating that it all feels so heavy. I don't know. Anyway, I'm discouraged. Terribly. I feel confused and upset as if all of this were doing no good. . ."

"Angry at me, too?"

"Well, I guess so. Why don't you help me more? I guess I do blame you when things don't go right. But," apologetically, "how can you perform miracles? . . .

"And Ken's been whining. Like a baby. He follows me, whining. Tags after me as if he were two. It drives me wild.

"When Ken whines, it's like that time he cried in his room because I'd shut him in there. Will he ever get over it? I feel I've done him irreparable harm. I've got to send him away. I'm sure I'm no good for him. I'm going to look into boarding schools. I talked with Vic about it this morning. I just can't keep the children with me. I can't."

That night Kenneth's asthma returned.

When he next came in to me, he was still wheezing. He was tight again. In his session he didn't want to do anything. He sat on my lap again like a baby until he finally told me he'd had a dream about his mother sending him back to Peoria to live for good with Grams and Gramps.

"That made you kind of mad at her, didn't it?"

He only shook his head, blocked.

Had he perhaps overheard his mother's conversation with his father over sending him away to school? Or had he possibly sensed her feelings? Or had he blown up in his fantasy whatever small hint she might have let drop?

I suggested, "Suppose we have a play with the puppets about your dream." But he didn't want to. He didn't want to *do* anything. He just sat on my lap and wanted me to hold him fast.

Cathy came in again, still depressed.

"I wish I were dead. I wish I'd never been born. I hate myself for what I've done to the children; for what I'm doing to them. Ken's having asthma again. I know it's me. I hate myself. I hate myself, too, for not being what Vic deserves. . ."

I noticed the tell-tale trembling of her hand and her eyes staring at the wall.

"There's something I've just seen. I haven't told you before because I hadn't told it to myself clearly. But I've been feeling it ever since my marriage. I see that now.

"I'm no good for Vic sexually. . .

"I told you sex was all right. Well, it is in that he has an orgasm and I have an orgasm. But, well, I don't have it naturally. I have to have him touch me. So he comes quickly so as not to get too tired. And then, afterward, he sees that I get satisfied.

"He could't be sweeter. But I know he can't like it. . . . It's . . . It's . . . It's . . . Well . . . as if I didn't like his penis. As if I preferred his hand.

"How could he be content with that? It's a kind of denial of his penis. As if I were still feeling what I felt toward it during pregnancy. Maybe that is the reason. Maybe I'm still angry at it for its having made me pregnant. Or maybe I'm still afraid it might make me pregnant again. But. . ." she paused, looking puzzled. "How can it be that? It's been the same all along, ever since we've been married—long before the children were born.

"I've been feeling so worthless. No good as a wife. No good as a mother. So helpless with the children..."

And then, with sudden shift from self-condemnation, "But there's one thing about Vic. He doesn't help me enough with the children. He doesn't give me enough support with them. He's just never there! He didn't want me to have them, so I've hated to demand anything from him. But boys do need a father, don't they?"

And without waiting for me to answer: "I think I'd better send him in to see you. Yes, I think that's a good idea."

TWELVE

Vic had been a basketball player in college. He was rangy. But the muscular look was gone. He was tall, but folded up on his tallness. He smiled shyly when he came in and dropped his eyes and bent his head so that the yellow crop of hair showed, a trifle darker than Ken's.

After our first mutual greetings, he sat down, crossed his legs, uncrossed, crossed the other leg over. He cleared his throat. "Cathy tells me I should consider myself a more important member of this combine, and that I should enter in more, if you know what I mean." His voice was without vibrance. A slow-droned monotone. As if the whole big man had been punctured and the vitality let out. "Cathy says what I do and what I am and what I do with her and the boys and what my family was like when I was little all count in Kenneth's problems. I guess they do. I've read some psychology. Where would you like me to begin?"

"Why don't you just take it in your own way, however you want."

He cleared his throat and swallowed. Uncrossed and recrossed those long legs with the knotty ankles. His wrists were knotty, and his arms were almost too long for his sleeves. His forehead also was knotted. His lids were half down, so that it was not till later that I noticed the very blue blue of his eyes, deep in their sockets like blue lakes sunken in mountain crevices too narrow to contain them. One never could quite come together in meeting with these very blue eyes. They never looked at you; always down or away.

"I think Cathy gives me credit for being better than I am. She blames herself too much for everything. I've always felt she had boundless possibilities if she could only believe in herself and not belittle herself so continuously. I think I'm not as much help as I should be. I'm too turned inward, if you know what I mean." He droned on in monotone without stopping but without ease. His tone, unresonant, was like Ken's tight whisper amplified into voice. "She feels I've done so much and I really haven't. I was top man in college. But take my work now. I think I should have gotten much further with it: I've got a good job and my boss is pleased with me, but somehow I don't get the promotions. I plod along and do what's expected and more, and I've often wished that Mr. Taylor—he's the head of the engineering firm I work for and he's been a kind of father to me—more than my own father, I think—I've often wished that he'd notice more and raise me or show other signs of appreciating the effort I put in and that I do the job well and don't get the firm into hot water the way some of the other boys do.

"Cathy thinks I should ask for a raise but I wouldn't want to do that; I think it's up to the boss to show his appreciation and anyway Mr. Taylor prefers the kind of man who doesn't push, though at times I do blame myself and think I'm too held back in myself. I've always had feelings of inadequacy, if you know what I mean . . ."

His words dragged on. He was like a gangly boy—fearful but trying in utmost conscientiousness to report everything with great honesty.

I wondered what had happened earlier to this good and intelligent person to so deplete him of aggressiveness and vitality.

Vic thought that Cathy's mother was too dominating. He objected also to her continuous criticism of Cathy. "It gets under my skin so I'm home as little as possible when I know she's going to be there." He was glad that Cathy was standing up for herself a little better and that she wasn't having her mother over so much. But he still found himself staying away from home more than he needed to or should. He didn't know why. He knew he shouldn't since it put the burden of the boys more heavily on Cathy's shoulders. "I think I put too much on Cathy anyway, if you know what I mean."

He swallowed and looked down. "I don't know why it is," recrossing his legs, "but our marriage isn't as happy as it should be. At least I don't think so, though I think Cathy does. She thinks the world and all of me. Too much, really. I'm not as wonderful as she thinks I am. Only it's a funny thing. I think I married her for that very reason. Because she thought I was so wonderful. I think that was a stronger reason why we were married than that I was in love with her. Sometimes I wonder how wholeheartedly I do love her. There's so much of me that doesn't belong to her. I'm turned inward so much; it's hard to share my inner thoughts with her. And yet I wouldn't want to leave her. She's important to me in a way I don't quite understand . . .

"My mother," shyly, "she used to think I was wonderful, too."

He was an only child. His father and mother had not gotten along well and his father had been away a lot from home. "I never got to know him well. He never got to know me well, either, nor to notice much what I did . . .

"He never was cross; never raised his voice. Neither did my mother but she was serious always and stern sometimes, and displeased in a quiet way that would make me feel more terrible than if she had given me a whipping. I'd slink out and go away from home and turn inward. I think in a way that I had to do more things than a boy my age should have to do to make up for my father's not being there . . .

"There's something else I think I should tell you." He swallowed hard and the Adam's apple on his thin neck went out and back. I felt he was groping for courage. And then he plodded in. "Cathy doesn't know it and I think it would make her unhappy, but I've had two affairs."

His persistent monotone let up for a moment. He sat with eyes lowered. Conscientiously he continued, "I thought you should know. I never had anything to do with any girl before we were married and I think I needed to make up for it or something. Both the girls were married. Both had had other lovers. Occasionally I still see Loretta. She's one of them. Pat's the other. Loretta's a particular friend of Cathy's and when she comes to town we always see her. I felt more alive somehow with them than with Cathy, with Loretta most of all . . ."

He went on to give me more details about them, contrasting Pat's fiery disposition with Cathy's contained air; and even more, contrasting Loretta's vivacity with Cathy's quietness. He felt he had been more passionately in love with them than ever with Cathy, more desirous of them, especially Loretta. Things had gone farthest with Loretta.

He went on persistently, dragging thoughts out. His tone never rose from its droning monotone. He was plodding forward and yet he was at the same time held back by an undertow of fear, as if there were some point he was trying to come to and yet to avoid.

And then, as if he must avoid it no longer, he put in something that came unexpectedly, still without change of tempo or tone.

"But I never consummated either affair." He smiled, shamefacedly unhappy. "I couldn't manage to, which was just as well. It kept me at home, if you know what I mean.

"And that brings me to another point—our sex life. Cathy said I should be sure to tell you about it. She blames herself constantly and I feel she shouldn't. There's nothing really to blame herself for, only she won't believe me when I tell her that. It's O.K. by me the way it is. In fact it's better, if you know what I mean."

And then, by way of explanation, "You see, I've never been able to hold out very long and this way it doesn't matter. I get satisfied and I can satisfy her all right, so I feel our sex relationship is all right. Only," he uncrossed his legs and sat forward a little, his big knees apart and the big hands with the knuckly wrists looking helpless between them, "sometimes I wish I wouldn't have to get it over with quite so fast!"

81

More than ever he seemed like a big, gangly and helpless youngster. And I felt that he was as afraid as was his own little boy of being a man.

THIRTEEN

Kenneth continued to wheeze till his next session in spite of
the fact that Cathy seemed heartened by Vic's having been
to see me.

She knew, of course, that what Vic told me was confidential
between him and me, and that my role was not to stand up for
either one or the other, nor to condemn either one to the other.
Nor was my role to act as judge or arbiter. Essentially, it was
to help each one, in so far as I could in the time available, to
get at his own feelings, so that gradually he might see himself
more honestly and freely. Then he would be able to see how
he could best relate himself to his family in ways that were
more honest and free.

Cathy reported that Ken's whining had stopped and his teasing also. He was once more the good, quiet little boy he'd been at the start. The quiet little boy with his asthma going strong.

Why was he closing up anew, I asked myself. Was it perhaps because he'd resented his father's coming to see me and feared to say it? Was it perhaps because of a recrudescence of resentment toward Cathy regenerated by her threat to send him away? Was he afraid that if he did things to displease her, she might go through with her threat? His dream about being sent again to his grandmother's, this time to stay, indicated that the latter possibility was at least on his mind.

He came and sat on my lap again and blew mouth bubbles. I called him my baby. And after a while I said I thought my baby was angry at something but wasn't saying so.

He shook his head and got down off my lap. Was he angry at me for having suggested that he was angry? Would he be afraid to show me? Or had my suggestion brought him fresh courage to go on, since by mentioning the possibility of his being angry I had given him sanction, as it were, to show it once more?

He began tentatively with the paints and with many hand-washings reminiscent of times past. Blue. Green. Finally brown.

Suddenly he pounced at me. Brown fingers spread in claw-like threat, almost into my face. His face hideous. His nose wrinkled up. His teeth bared.

More brown on his hands. More pouncing claws striking into the air in my direction. Brown on the stick with which he had been stirring the paint. Brown, thick on the paper.

"Yips! I'll mix more brown."

He took the wooden spatula and stirred the paint. "Iggh;

igghy. Gwush; gwushy." And then, with a sudden move, he threw the spatula. Toward me. But short.

He grinned. Broad and free. The tightness was gone. And so was the asthma. Kenneth's wheezing had stopped.

To myself I commented that never once had I needed to restrict Kenneth as I did some children. However if Ken had actually tried to hit me, I would have restrained him. For a pretended or imaginary attack is one thing. It can ultimately be countered by the knowledge that the attack was not real. But as soon as an attack is made on a physical level, it acquires the potentiality of actual hurt. In its turn, actual hurt holds the possibility of taking away the person who is struck. It can terrify the child with a fear of losing that person and with guilt over having been the cause.

Ken had not actually touched me even though his intent was clear. His hostility was again open. He had pounced and thrown the brown stick in my direction. Quite unconcerned now, he retrieved the spatula and mixed and splattered and messed some more.

I said, "I think you wanted to throw the spatula at me."

He grinned again. "You silly Mother. You silly Dorothy."

Again there had been the unconscious slip. It was not at me he'd aimed in his mind; but at his mother. Both in his therapy and at home he had, on the whole, held back on whatever hostility he might have felt toward her. He was using me now in her place. Nonetheless it was me he'd gone after.

"You wanted to go after me with the stick."

"Uhuh!" he nodded, very pleased. And in complete affirmation, "Yes, I did."

When he went out, he still was free of the wheezing, and he stayed clear at home.

Very shortly after this, an interesting thing happened. On his way in, Kenneth ran into an older boy with whom I'd just been working who was just going out.

Ken took a hunk of clay and spanked it vigorously. Then, looking up, he asked, "What was that boy's name?"

"Bob."

"Did he do things with you?"

"Yes."

"What did he do?"

"Made pictures."

"I want to make pictures too. I'll make a better one than Bob."

He started to draw with the crayons.

"You haven't been playing with Bob as long as you've been playing with me, have you?"

"I don't think you like me to play with Bob at all."

"No, I don't."

Then, after a few minutes, deciding for himself in accordance with the wish inside him, "I've been here longer than Bob," with evident relish.

But presently his smile disappeared, beaten back by some unspoken fantasy. "Bob doesn't like me to come here, does he?"

Quickly, however, he glossed this over as if he were wishing that it had been unthought. "What did Bob draw?"

"What would you guess?"

"I don't know."

"Think a bit!"

"We-ell, I think he drew about something he was mad about."

"Like what?"

"We-ell. Now I'll have to think double. I'll have to think

what he drew and what he was mad about. Yesterday I was mad 'cause a bigger boy took my kite away from me."

Worry shadowed across his face. "Did Bob's father take something away from him?"

"What do you think?"

"Yes. But what? Yes," querulous, "his father took something away from him. But I don't know what. I think he took somebody away from Bob."

"Like you thought Bob sort of took me away from you when he played with me?"

He nodded. "Yes. Only fathers take mothers away from their boys." His voice dropped. "They take them to bed. Sometimes . . ." And again quickly, as if moving to more comfortable territory, "I'm drawing a battle. A battle with an enemy plane. I can fight. I can."

It was time to stop, but in his next session he wanted to go on with the picture. He wanted to make it better than Bob's.

He had two planes in it. A big plane and a little plane fighting over a ship below.

As he drew the little plane, he sang,

> "I want to be a mean me,
> Not a little me,
> But a mean old me.
> A *big* mean me.
> That's what I am."

But, alas, the valiant attempt went wrong. The little plane could not vanquish the big one. "The big plane hit the little one and exploded it into a million burns."

He sat for a moment, thinking. "I'll draw another thing."

This time it was a picture of his brother. And this time he did the destroying. "I'll scrabble him, scrabble him, smash him up."

And another picture. This time of Grams. She too got scrabbled and scrabbled and smashed. He ground his teeth. "I'm a mean old me. A mean old me, and I'm having a wonderful time!"

Whether he had been too violent in the thoughts that accompanied this inwardly, or whether he wanted proof of my loving him in spite of his big meanness, I don't know. But he got up from the floor and climbed on my lap. He snuggled down for a few minutes, his thumb in his mouth.

"You're still my baby, sometimes," I said, hugging him. And presently, laughing, "And sometimes you're a big mean me."

He sat up, laughing with me. "And you can be *my* baby," he said.

I nodded.

Ken turned imperious. "You get down on the floor."

I did.

"Now crawl over here, my little baby. Crawl over here to me and put your hand on my knee."

I did while he sat regally, looking down at me and pulling himself up as tall as he could.

And then, with a sudden, swift movement, he picked up my hand, lifted it to his mouth and kissed it. And his face broke into a smile which, although soundless, seemed to me to be chuckling like a small bright breeze.

Through making me smaller, Kenneth had been able to make himself bigger. Big enough not to be defensively consumed with hate. Sitting there, blond crowned, like a king, he was big enough to be a man. To be like a father, showing me love.

FOURTEEN

He smiled with obvious affection when he next came in and again when he went out. He did show-off stunts, acting silly. He teased me giddily. Taking the toy telephone out, "See, it fell over. The phone won't work. Ah phooey! It's stuck! Ahgah! I gotta getta numbah. Ya yah, hello! It's going rrrurrr rurrrruhr. Hello, hello. Gish, ishy goo. I got to dial uggie. My goodness. Hello, Hello. Goodbye. Goodbye." Or, putting things away in the cupboard, "See, Dorothy, what happened? The box won't close. It's absolutely impossible to close it!" Meanwhile closing it easily with a twist of his hand.

He played in water. And more water. And more water still. He ran water into the basin. Dipped his hand in. Dripped water out from the medicine dropper. Took a large syringe that I'd begged from the doctor and filled it. Squirted it into buckets and bowls. He made holes in clay and squirted water into these.

"Does that boy Bob squirt as good as I do?

"Do any other boys come in to play with you?"

I answered, "I think you'd rather no other boys would."

"We-ell," he said, "I'm not the selfish type. But maybe . . . we-ell, I would just once in a while like to be your onliest child!"

He made brothers and smashed them.

Water and more water. The holes now were to put things into. What went in seemed almost more important than the hole. Water particularly. His emphasis was not on the holes themselves now. Not on their passive receptiveness. Not, as formerly, on how the holes felt. His attention was now on the going in.

"Water, water going in. Squirt it. Squirt."

He turned on the faucet full force. "The water runs from the spout. It runs in the bowl!"

Water and more water. Spouts. Faucets. Syringes. All splashing and spraying and squirting.

Until finally the meaning came clear.

"Splatter, splatter, dribble, dribble. Splatter, splatter, I can splash. I can make a dent in the sink. I can wet with my penis, too. I can wet into any old hole."

At last the wish was out in the open. Kenneth did want to have a penis. He wanted not only to claim its possession, but to claim it as a usable part of his body, to use as a man with a woman, the awareness of its use rising out of some primitive knowledge and out of what else? What might he have heard? What might he have seen?

This went beyond the brown big job penis. This claimed a phallus, or, as he later made the distinction, "a front penis rather than a back penis." This went beyond the safety of father with daughter, hemmed in neatly by our cultural taboos. He was showing himself to me as a male, as a man, not to a child but to a wife.

He was showing me this for this moment. But it was too young. Too new. Too difficult. Too frightening. It could not last long.

As he started to work with the finger paints, he noticed that the sponge with which he dampened the paper had been used earlier. It was still wet. When he squeezed it, the water oozed out, tinged with red paint.

I noticed his recoil and remembered his earlier recoil when he'd gotten a bit of red on his fingers from the cover of the paint jar.

He picked up the sponge gingerly now, carried it to the sink and started to wash it. He must wash out all the red. Thoroughly. "Is it clean? Is it clean?" Obviously he was anxious. Only after he could squeeze the water from the sponge and see that there was no trace of red left did he go back to his painting. And then he used pale colors only and he painted half-heartedly. Silent, until presently a curious train of thought lifted the silence off his tongue.

He spoke of his father. It was as if his mind had leaped from the sponge to that other boy who might have used it with me, and from him to his father. And he began speaking of what his father had done to him. "My father gave me a haircut. But I didn't want him to cut my hair. He might cut too much."

Then turning back to the paints, he made his fingers move

up and down, up and down. "Here comes an earthquake." He looked frightened.

Then quickly, as if to intercept fear, he announced, "My father likes me. He's not an angry man. I helped him stamp envelopes and he gave me two stamps. Only when I went to find them he'd taken them away." He drew his pale eyebrows together. "Well, anyway they were gone."

To myself I remarked on the sequence:

Red paint.

Shock.

Father cutting.

Fear that his father might cut too much.

The catastrophe of an earthquake.

The attempt to comfort himself with the fact that his father was not an angry man, and the attempt to please his father by helping him with the stamps and to further reassure himself that his father gave things to him.

And finally, the worry: his losing something and his father taking it away.

Then he went back to messing. Resentful and angry. Brown and more brown. Brown hunks falling. He continued this play until he seemed calmer. Again he was a baby, retreating from maleness to the "brown penises" that he could store inside.

Then he did another curious thing. He got a piece of string. Rolled out a roll of clay. Took the string and, using the string like a saw, he sliced the clay roll. "I'm magic. I'm slicing it up without any hurting. I'm slicing off all the sticking-out pieces.

"I'm slicing bread. I'm slicing meat. Lots and lots of things. Remember how big it stuck out? Now there's almost nothing left."

He kept on slicing till the roll was gone.

He surveyed his accomplishment seriously. Then, like an old man shaking his head over a sad but inevitable happening, he said quite factually, "Whosoever this little boy is, he doesn't have any more head. And he doesn't have any more penis. Poor little boy."

Something about red and father and cutting had frightened him. He had chosen to do the cutting himself. Without hurt. As if by magic. Like preferring to take out one's own splinter. The lesser of two evils, since the evil to him so apparently seemed a necessity of circumstance or of fate.

FIFTEEN

He was an angry boy after this. Openly angry at me. And he had no asthma. It was as if he were resenting and expressing his resentment over not feeling able to acknowledge his maleness.

He kept messing and bombing. Mostly brothers, but sometimes fathers, grandfathers, grandmothers. Mothers were for the most part immune. Even in his play he could not yet freely reveal feelings toward mothers. But he did keep on using me as a target for his mother-directed hostility. He kept playing that he was attacking me with clawing fingers and brown-smeared sticks.

In addition he kept slicing off roll after roll of clay,

94

quietly demolishing them. But it seemed to me that gradually some reluctance crept in.

He had tried in various ways to gain a male organ; to have more than a hole like a girl. He had finally gotten the brown penis. This was his present solution. But he had been able to declare, even though only during the flash of a moment, his definite wish to have more. Was he going to gather fresh impetus now?

I waited, hoping that he would try to solve his dilemma and wondering what sort of solution he would seek.

One day, not long after, it came.

He started to talk of his father, of having been fishing with him the day before. "I ate a fish my father caught. A whopper. A big one. As big as an elephant's trunk. I ate it . . ."

Mischievously he put some clay in his mouth.

"I'll eat it. Mmmmmm. Father's fish!"

He was eating something that belonged to father. Eating something of father's like a baby eats something of mother's to grow on. Only this thing of father's was big. "Big as an elephant trunk," he went on to say. And so, as if the bigness were magic and gave him some secret bigness of his own—as if it gave him some magic strength, he came back next session and immediately went to the red paint jar. He lifted it. Looked at it. Paused.

This was the first time he had chosen red. And he'd been scared of the sponge with its red ooze such a short time before. Would he dare bring the jar out? Would he have enough courage to tackle that which he feared about red? Or would he put the red jar back on the shelf and retreat?

He stepped out, the red paint jar still in his hand. He unscrewed the cover. He started to work.

I knew from other children that when they finally came to

tackle something they feared in this way, they were daring the danger it stood for. They were trying to cope with that danger. Trying to meet it. Like a person frightened by night noises daring to look out into the dark instead of tucking head under covers. I knew, too, that only by straightforward looking could the absence of danger be proven. Only through tackling the fear could the fear disappear.

He smeared the red paint over the paper. Over his fingers. Over his hands.

"I have bloody hands." Very sober.

He splashed the red paint. "I'm getting blood all over me." He streaked it up his arm.

He covered the paper with red and stippled it with patting palms.

That was all for now. But at least he'd had courage to approach and not retreat from whatever blood meant.

That this did give him courage became apparent next time. He chose clay.

He made "a snake."

"This is my snake. I got him in the garden. He sleeps in my bed. Nobody knows I have him. Just you and me. He curls up and he uncurls and stretches." He himself stretched up tall.

But the imagined fear of injury swiftly followed this idea.

"You know, my arm the other day, last time I was here? It was red. And my picture? It looked like scars where I patted it. See, I have scars on my arm."

He stretched his arm out for me to see. The scars now were barely discernible. I might never have noticed them had the doctor not told me at the beginning that Kenneth's arm had been burned.

"It happened when I was little. We had a folding stool and I stood on it and was watching some eggs boil and the steam coming out of the pot. And I guess I held my hand out to feel the steam 'cause I was cold and it was warm. Only the stool fell over and I lost my balance and hit the pot and my arm almost burned off."

He grew very pensive. "That was before Mother sent me away to Peoria." He turned slowly, picked up the piece of string and began slicing his snake.

I asked, "Did you think she sent you because what you did was bad?"

He looked up at me a moment. His blond brows came to gether. Everything paused. His thoughts seemed to hang in mid-air.

Then he said something surprising.

"Doctors hurt you too, like dogs."

Seriously he returned to slicing.

"They cut things. My tonsils. They cut my tonsils last year."

More slicing.

"Dorothy? Did you ever have a dog with a stubby tail?"

I nodded, waiting.

"Doctors cut tails off of some dogs when they're little. Like my dog, Hamburger. But I don't see what for."

It was then he made a telling gesture. His hand moved down unwittingly toward his crotch as if in a self-protecting move.

"It makes you scared," I ventured, "to think of the doctor cutting things off."

He nodded. "When they cut my tonsils I was asleep. Sometimes I dream in my sleep that I'll get something cut off. My mother had something cut off. She had an operation."

Again the puzzled drawing together of brows.

"My mother . . . She had . . . I forgot what she had cut off. It was . . . App . . . A pp . . . A *penis?* . . .A penis. That's what they cut off her. No, an appendix. Yes, that's it. They cut it 'cause Grams was mad at her and Gramps, too. She was bad."

Unwittingly again, he clutched at his penis.

"Grams got mad at me too."

His hand was still at his crotch.

"She said she'd cut something off you?" I asked.

"We-ell, she says if you touch it, your penis . . ." he left the sentence hanging and picked it up confusedly, "Gramps will . . . Grams says . . . Mother says . . ." And then, "But she hardly ever sees me . . ."

"When she does," I said softly, "tell me, what does she say?"

"She says, 'Don't touch your penis.' "

"And that's real scary," I nodded. "But silly."

He looked at me, questioningly.

"Some people think that sort of thing," I said. "But I think it's silly. It feels good to touch your penis. And it isn't bad."

He breathed a great sigh. A wide smile spread across his face. Beatific. He looked as relieved as though some stinging insect had suddenly flown off, surprisingly leaving no pain. He got up and came over to me and put his hand on my cheek very softly.

"We had a barbecue last night," he confided. "I was afraid to get close to the fire. Maybe *it* would get burned like my arm did. If I got too close."

"Or, if you touch it and make it feel warm and good like fire?"

"Uhhum. Grams said it would burn off like my arm almost did."

"But it won't. Nothing bad really happens when you touch it and make it feel warm and good."

"Not really?" reaching for truth.

"Not really, though sometimes you think in your thoughts that it might."

When he left at the end of the session, the shyness was gone as if a great fear had been lifted. For the moment at least.

SIXTEEN

It all came out more clearly in subsequent sessions. Kenneth's impression was that Grams had told him that if he touched himself she'd have to get Gramps to cut off his penis. It was bad to touch oneself. So bad that even though she and Gramps never found out, still God would see and He would punish Ken. He might cause some accident to occur like the burn on Ken's arm.

Mother had been bad. She'd done something bad and Grams had gotten the doctor to cut off mother's penis. Or at least a part of her penis. Ken could not see if it was all gone or not. "Part of it might be buried in that fuzz. Or it might be hiding up inside her somewhere." The place where it had been cut off still bled sometimes.

As for this last, Cathy told me that a while back Ken had come across one of her pads. She had explained to him that babies grow inside the mother and that while the babies are growing the mother's blood feeds them. But if there's no baby inside the mother, the blood comes out every so often. But Ken's own inner interpretation was more convincing to him. The blood came from the place where mother had been cut.

He wished mother hadn't been cut. He wished her ears stuck out like noses. He didn't like anything that seemed cut off. And yet, bumps were even more frightening. Every protuberance carried the danger of some potential cut-off-ness that could be more terrible than that which had already been done. Feet could be amputated, legs injured, like on the wounded soldier who would never get well. It was easier to see the world "bump-less," without any protrusions. Big jobs were the only ones that were safe. They could be hidden inside, for one thing, and furthermore they could be reproduced ad infinitum. If one was destroyed, there were lots and lots more.

But he did like to use his penis to wet and he did like to touch it. And he didn't like Grams for telling him it was bad. That was certain.

He took out the small dolls who represented various family members and played that a boy whose name was Sam had a grandma who scolded him. "What she said, though, is just a bunch of silly ideas, isn't it?"

"Yes," I answered. "But lots of people have those silly ideas. Lots of times you still have them too, don't you?"

He nodded, meanwhile making the grandmother trip over the toilet.

101

"You think she's naughty," I said, "to have those scary ideas!"

"Yes. I don't like her 'cause she tells lies. She tells lies about the penis. We'll drown her in the toilet and close the toilet on her. She told lies about cutting Sam's penis off. We'll put her head in the toilet so she can't talk any more. We'll make her blind."

"So she can't see any more what you like to do?"

"Uhuh," with an appreciative chuckle.

But killing Grams off didn't solve the problem. Nor did the ray of hope I gave in letting him know that I didn't think he was bad. This last helped, yes. But he had a long way to go. He would have to explore and play out and play over and over, in one context and another, all the various parts of the picture. He would have to uncover ramifications and unexplored fears not yet seen. He would probably relive further thoughts left as hang-overs from the earlier childhood-thoughts that all small children have and lose as the logic and conscience of growing-up catch hold.

I had made no attempt to change Kenneth's vocabulary from his infant terms to more scientific ones. He himself had used "penis." So I too would use this word as I would also use with him the more infantile terms in which he was wont to think of other bodily parts and processes. I wanted to stay with whatever terms were most familiar to him. For feelings can best be brought out in the words to which they have become attached. Just as it is harder to bring out deeper thoughts and feelings in a foreign language, so adult terms—foreign to Kenneth—might hamper him. Since Kenneth's feelings concerning these things were still infantile I would not try to disengage them from the language of infancy in which he most comfortably expressed his thoughts.

Bizarre though they were, Kenneth's thoughts were natural child thoughts and as illogical and full of fantasy as are all children's. From the vantage point of adult logic, they looked as strangely distorted as images seen in the mirrors of fun-houses.

I knew that as Kenneth dragged them out and felt them through with me beside him, as he played them out again and again and saw that I still loved and accepted him, he might eventually come to see that they did not need to bring terror. And this was essential. For Kenneth's trouble did not lie in possessing these thoughts which all children possess. It lay in his having locked them in along with fear and shame as such fell companions that it necessitated far too much energy keeping the barricades guarded and shut.

Would Kenneth be able to withstand the fear that these thoughts and feelings held for him? Would he have enough courage to go on? And would his parents have enough courage to let him? Or, would they, like some other parents I'd seen, become too frightened? Would they find it too difficult to accept new things in Kenneth? Temporary over-aggressiveness, perhaps, until he struck a balance? Temporary silliness or what not? Or would new things emerging in Kenneth perhaps touch off old, forgotten feelings inside of themselves? And would his father and mother, then, pushed by their own archaic fears, take Kenneth out of therapy too soon before the gains had become permanent and secure?

I had grown to have great confidence in Cathy's ability to take things. But I knew that some problems might still prove beyond endurance. Such a one soon arose.

As Kenneth's courage came through, his interest in being a boy returned. He began wetting games with his brother in the bathroom, and one night Cathy thought she detected him touching himself in bed. Outwardly Cathy gave lip service to seeing the thing as a natural, childish act, well nigh universal. Nonetheless, inner fears dating back to her own childhood were set off.

When she was little she had touched herself too.

"Mother would tell me I'd better be good. If I didn't quit, terrible things would happen. I'd be put away in an institution. Or she would have to be put away because I was driving her insane.

"I'd never grow up normal. I'd never be able to have children normally. I'd never be able to lead a normal, happy life."

Anxiety slid in as silently as a dark snake through pond grass. Cathy's hands trembled. The thin skin drew tauter across her forehead. Her eyes darkened as an old terror crept out.

"Do you think that's why I have to have Vic touch me now? Because I used to do it? No. No. It couldn't be. I've read what the books say. My mother was wrong. She wasn't right, was she?"

Like Kenneth, she was trying to convince herself that Grams didn't know or that Grams had told lies.

And then, guilty because she was trying so hard to disprove her mother and because of the web of spidery strands stickily clinging to the thought that was central, she began to lose courage.

"I'm afraid I haven't given you a true picture of my mother. I've just told you the bad things about her. I feel so ashamed. She's the way I should be. A good housewife. Industrious. Charitable. She helps at church bazaars. She puts up fruit. She sews for me and the children. I've not been fair to her. Truly, I've not been fair."

Her mother was good. She, Cathy, was bad. In a surge of appeasement, she asked her mother over more frequently. She asked Vic for money to help her mother buy curtains. She asked Vic to take her mother driving. She asked Vic to fix the peeling paint on the garage which her mother criticized.

Vic said, "All right." But he failed to get around to it. He was too busy. He was never at home.

And then one day Loretta came to visit Cathy. She had been in town for a couple of weeks and had spoken to Cathy several times on the telephone, but this was her first opportunity to visit. They sat and talked and talked. Loretta's smile flashed vivaciously through her red-lipped pout. Her laugh rose readily as she tossed back her platinum, shoulder-length bob.

The chatter was of this and that. Cathy's therapy, Cathy's children. Loretta's new boy friend, Jim, and her recent divorce. The ice in their high-ball glasses clicked in chuckling accompaniment. Suddenly, with a flick of her cigarette and an unwonted stillness that sent her hair in straight falling lines at each side of her face, Loretta murmured, "Perhaps I shouldn't tell you, Cathy. But Vic's been over to see me at my hotel . . ."

Cathy stared. Dark eyes darker. The ice danced in earthquaking giddiness with her trembling.

Loretta went on. "He's written to me too. This letter, Cathy. I thought you should know." And vaguely, "We've been friends so long."

The paper quivered as Cathy read Vic's note to Loretta. It was pathetically adolescent. In spite of herself Cathy saw this. Two lines stood out: Vic was happy only in Loretta's presence. He remembered what had once been and hoped it might be once more.

105

"I've told you, Cathy, I'm going to marry Jim. I don't want Vic. Though once I did. Only nothing happened, Cathy. Nothing really. Only I thought you should know.

"I found with my own first marriage, Cathy, that a marriage can't be broken into unless there's already a breach. You can cover it up and say everything's fine. Only it's still there and it catches up with you eventually. I don't know what's wrong in your marriage, Cathy. Only I hate to see anything happen really. You and Vic and the two children, you've got each other and something worth working to keep. You say you're doing something about yourself. I think Vic should too."

That night Cathy asked Vic about it.

"I couldn't keep it under. You can see that! It was such a relief to have it out. Now that it's all in the open, I think I've always known. And Vic told me about Pat too."

She was calm. She was quiet. Holding steady and tight. Relieved, she said, to know everything. I looked ahead in my mind's eye, wondering when the storm would come.

Cathy wanted desperately to have Vic have some psychotherapy. There were several husbands and wives together in the group psychotherapy sessions to which Cathy came. These and some occasional individual sessions for Vic as he felt a particular need for talking alone were all they could afford to add now to what they were already handling. Would the doctor and I let Vic come into the psychotherapy group?

Vic came to see me several days later and re-voiced Cathy's request. Like Cathy, he felt relief to have things in the open though he had been surprised and hurt over what Loretta had done. He knew he needed help. He knew he needed to be less drawn into himself. He knew he needed to be able to stay at home more and not "pull out" as soon as things grew disagree-

106

able. He knew if he could be more supportive to Cathy that she would be better able to cope with her mother. All these things he knew.

The doctor and I talked the situation over. We chose carefully the few married couples we had in group therapy together. Several had made good progress. However, to let them come in together we had to feel that there was a chance of ultimate cohesiveness between them and we had to feel that their mutual revealing of feelings held the potentiality of calling forth reactions that would eventually bring into being a more alive and genuinely responding relationship. After much discussion between us, we decided that we would agree to Vic's and Cathy's request. Vic became part of the therapy group.

As we worked along through the next months, Kenneth went over and over, in differing versions, what he had been showing to me. He had bad moments and good ones as far as his progress was concerned. Every once in a while he would close up, sometimes for a shorter, sometimes for a longer period. I came to see that this happened most when he was feeling an upsurge of hostility to his mother and was unable to let it come through. And this he was still not able to do readily. His eyes would dull. His shoulders would droop. The brightness would leave him. His breath would turn rasping and the sound of his voice would turn muted and low.

Although he still could not come out strong and direct with any hostility to his mother, when we could get out hostile feeling against me as a substitute mother or against his father, when he was involved, the asthma would clear.

Sometimes we could do this in one session, as on the day after Cathy had reported having felt tremendous revulsion toward Ken for trying to give her an Eskimo kiss, rubbing his nose playfully against hers.

She had been able to be frank. "In spite of myself, I felt such utter disgust. Something about his nose reminded me of the part of men I like least."

He had not wheezed immediately when she recoiled. But Ken had an asthma attack that night after she and Vic had gone to bed.

"As if he wanted to get me away from Vic," Cathy smiled knowingly and a little vindictive, she went on. "In addition, he did disturb my sleep."

Kenneth came in dejected. Wheezing. He spoke again in a half-voice, hardly above a whisper. He wanted again to sit on my lap and be accepted as my baby.

Finally, feeling somewhat reassured but still wheezing, Kenneth took out some clay.

"I'll make a teeny tiny peanut boy. A nothing. A puppet. Then I can do anything I want to him."

He demolished the teeny, tiny puppet with rising vigor. "There," he said, "that's the brother puppet. Now I'll make a great big puppet."

This he did and attacked the big figure with real fury. "Big old mean thing. Big old mean thing. I'm spanking him and tearing him up."

He laughed without the trace of a wheeze. "I spanked him so hard I'll have blisters before I know it. And I cut him right down the middle. And now I'll put him in the garbage. So there."

He had been angry at his mother for her recoil over his loving gesture. However he had not been able to direct the anger frankly at her. But he had gotten out anger against his father. And in his mind this was closely connected with his not hav-

108

ing his mother. Fcr, as he had said earlier, "Fathers take mothers away from their boys. They take them to bed."

It was as if he were skirting around the center and as if the center contained his mother and a hard swollen core of resentment toward her. I knew that sooner or later the core would need to be gone at directly. As long as it stayed hidden, Kenneth would not be cured.

This time the hostility had come out very quickly. But at other times it seemed almost endless before we could glimpse and get out what was there.

On the whole, though, Kenneth was more open and the asthma was much less than before he had started. We knew, for one thing, from its recurrences that he still had a long road ahead, and that he had not worked out enough in his sessions to carry over into his day-to-day life.

As for the school: The end of the year came and Kenneth got his promotion. The principal called me. "I told you we wouldn't have to demote him. Scholastically he's done very well. I can tell you with certainty that he's far from dumb. I'm waiting though till next year to test him. He's still pretty closed in. He still steers clear of the children at recess. He doesn't want to play games. He goes to the nurse's office sometimes to get out of them. He lacks aggressiveness both in his work and in his social relations. He's no superman when it comes to fighting his own battles or getting the other youngsters to give him a chance."

Another thing that had happened which seemed to please Ken was that his parents had given him a room of his own instead of continuing to have him share one with his brother. "It's been our study," said Cathy ruefully. "But I guess if it's good for him, we can stand it."

109

In his therapy sessions his interest in water play kept increasing. There was much use of syringes, droppers, tubes. Much dripping and squirting, until one day he enacted a fight. "It's a fight between the wee-wee and the big job. The wee-wee covers the big job and washes it away."

He was serious and pensive. "The front penis did better than the back penis today."

He went on to tell me that his mother had made him take his lunch to school instead of coming home. The other boys, he said wistfully, sat under a pergola outside on the playground and ate. But, hanging his head, he'd eaten his sandwiches inside in the school room because he didn't think the boys wanted him with them. "Do you think, Dorothy?" with a ray of hope showing, "do you think, maybe someday they will?"

It was as if the thought of having a boy's equipment had brought with it a kind of looking forward to being a boy with other boys. He didn't yet dare. But something was happening.

Finger painting later, he asked me to look at him. He made constrained, stiff movements with his finger tips on the paper as if he were putting on an act.

"Look, Dorothy, how slow I am."

A grin of amusement crept across his face. "Remember, I used to be like that?"

Then, in swift transition, his hands swept back and forth over the sheet in full-armed, sweeping gesture, wide and free.

"See, Dorothy! I'm not that way any longer. Now I'm like this."

SEVENTEEN

As Kenneth worked on, a major stream of thought crossed the horizon into clearer view and etched its way through time: Things went into holes and hollows.

Bombs fell into craters. Rain streamed into boats and barrels. Water ran into mouths. And wee-wee squirted into this and that and "any old hole."

In turn questions came bubbling up from crevices and ran as tributaries from the main current: "What happens *in* there after the water goes in?" pointing to a water-drenched hole in a mound of clay... "What comes out?" In his mind there was a picture of something going in, of its being transformed, and of its coming out. "When the food goes in the mouth, what

111

happens in here?" touching his stomach. "It grows into big jobs and brother big jobs. It changes. And it comes out the big job hole."

And still another question: "Do some things burst when some things come out?"

He drew a picture with crayons of a father plane flying overhead. Underneath was a house where a mother lived. The father plane dropped a brown bomb right into the mother's chimney. Only, as it touched the chimney it turned into a great big fire-bomb. Red and burning. Once inside the house it started a conflagration. Flames filled the house. The steam in the house grew bigger and had to get out some way. And finally, with a tremendous blast, the house exploded into a million bits.

Something going in. Something being transformed. Something coming out. How?

I was not surprised when Kenneth tied these questions together one day, showing that they had in truth been fantasies and wonderings about impregnation and birth.

His guppies, he said, had too many babies.

"The babies come out from the mother guppies' stomachs. From their stomachs somewhere. But I don't know from just where. I've never examined a guppy that close."

He drew his eyebrows together and sat as if trying to solve some great riddle. "I wonder what hole they come out of, those baby guppies?" And quickly another question hit its toes on the heels of this last. "I wonder," more slowly, "I wonder where *we* come out of? What hole?"

"What would be your guess?" I asked him.

"What hole?" figuring. "Now what hole could it be? Let me see. Could it be the wee-wee hole?" His hand moved toward his own body as if he were trying to solve the question in terms of himself. "No! The wee-wee hole isn't big enough. Could it be the big job hole? Let me see. No! The big job hole, that's bigger but it still isn't big enough. Not for a real live baby to come out of. No hole's big enough." And then, quizzically, "Is there another hole?"

I knew from way back that he knew it, but he needed me to put it into words for him now.

"Not on a man," I said. "But there is on a woman."

"Oh!" he exclaimed, with the light breaking through in the brilliance of discovery. "She's got a *baby* hole! Oh, I see!"

He repeated the cherished finding. "She's got three holes! A wee-wee hole. A big job hole. And a baby hole. That's what that other hole's for."

Then again thoughtful, "I'd like to know, Dorothy, how does the baby come out of the baby hole? Does the mother come apart?"

It was near the end of the session so I told him that we could have a clay mother and make her have a baby next time. Then he could see how the baby got out.

"Make her be a real fat mother," he requested. "With a baby inside."

I nodded and we both chuckled in anticipation.

He started to leave, well satisfied.

Suddenly, however, half-way to the door, an important thought struck him. "But how about the father? And how does the baby get *in*? Babies need fathers, too, don't they?"

"Yes, of course babies need fathers, and we can have a father here too next time!"

"That's good!" He beamed satisfaction. "We'll have a father, too. And then we can see what *he* does."

When he came in for his next session the ripely rounded mother was waiting for him. Inside her body lay a cardboard baby, curved, head down, waiting to be born. The father, beside the mother, looked sturdily possessive.

Kenneth eyed them, smiling. Presently he picked up the mother and nodded approvingly, "She surely is big and fat."

He examined her in detail. "Oh, yes, I see the wee-wee hole, that's this one. And I see the big job hole, that's this one. I guess, then, that this one here is the baby hole. Is that where she's going to have the baby from?" And without waiting for an answer, "I wonder will it be a boy or a girl?"

"Which do you think?"

"Me? I don't know. I'm no mind reader. Come on, we'd better make her have it and see."

So without more ado, we had the father get her to the hospital and with me as doctor, and him as chief assistant, we readily helped the baby come out.

He picked it up, looked it over, and muttered, disgustedly, "Oh, it's a boy."

But his main concern was for the mother. He was manipulating her, changing her form, thinning her down.

"There," with a satisfied air, "there she is now. She hasn't got that big monster tummy any more. But she has got big things for the baby to stick his face into and drink from."

The baby was at last in the mother's arm, its face at her breast.

"See, Mister," turning to the father. "You've got a baby boy."

Then to me, "What did the father do? How did he help?"

Inadvertently or intentionally, I did not know which, his hand touched the clay man's genitals.

I nodded. "You're showing me the right thing just at the

right moment. I think you knew what the father helps with to make the baby."

He nodded slyly, grinning broadly, very pleased. Then, almost garrulously, he rattled off what his mother had read to him earlier from one of the books she had gotten. "The father has a seed. It's very, very, very tiny. And he plants it in the mother. And first it looks like a seed and then a pollywog and then a fish and then a monkey and then it gets bigger and looks like a real baby after a long long time."

We took tiny bits of clay and made mother seeds and father seeds and welded them together to get the idea that mother and father each contribute half the seed for the new baby to grow from. "They weld together all in one and the baby starts." And with a kind of defiant decisiveness, "The mother *does* need the father to get a baby."

Then his eyebrows puckered. "But tell me, Dorothy, where does the father get his seed from? Does he keep it in his stomach? Or in his penis? Or where?"

"From quite near there," I commenced. But before I could finish, he anticipated me, "Oh, from here!" pointing down at himself. "From those balls."

"Yes."

"Oh, dear." His face fell. "Oh, dear." His voice trailed dejectedly, "Oh, dear, that's too bad!"

"Why?" I queried.

"Because," he answered, disconsolate, "I wanted a *lot* of children, but if they come from there *I can only have two*."

I assured him that even though there were only two balls, there were millions and millions of baby seeds in each.

"Millions and millions!" he exclaimed, very pleased. "Then I could have millions and millions of babies. That is, if I lived long enough."

115

"And you would have to live a very long time," I said. "Each baby, you know, takes nine months to grow."

"I know. And besides, millions would be too expensive. Children *are* expensive, by the time you get them chops and stew and suits and shoes."

We pondered for some minutes on the economic problems of raising a family. And then Kenneth, glancing at the father, went back to biological concerns. "Now, how does the father's seed get out of the father?"

"How would you guess?"

He looked knowing. "Through here. Through the wee-wee hole?"

"Yes, you knew it."

He nodded. "I guess I'm kind of a good guesser," self-satisfied. "I think it comes up from the seed bag in the balls here and out the wee-wee hole."

"Yes," I nodded. "And then? What do you think?"

"I think, then it goes into the mother's baby hole. Here," pointing. And half to himself, wonderingly, "How does it get there? Well, I guess the father has to bring it there with his penis."

I nodded again.

"O.K. Let's play the baby they had is two years old now and they want another baby. You show me how the father gets it there." As he talked he pushed the cardboard baby back up inside the mother, then seriously handed the father to me, and laid the mother on her back. "Now you show me."

Just as seriously I laid the father on the mother with his arms around her and hers around him in mutual embrace, body to body in the way of man and woman since the time of Adam and Eve.

116

Kenneth's face was beatific. "They love each other, that father and mother."

Then he peered under the father so as to see all the better. He regarded them from every possible angle and smiled as if he, like Pippa, felt that all was right with the world.

"The father puts his penis right in the baby hole and now the baby's started and they're loving each other."

"And sometimes," I said, "they do it just for love because too many babies would be too expensive, as we said."

"This time, though, they're doing it for a baby," he decided. "There, now it's done."

He lifted the father off.

"Lady, you're going to have a baby," he announced.

To me he said, "Now he's done it and the baby's starting." And then he voiced a strange request which I did not immediately comprehend.

"Dorothy, now you say, 'One month.' "

"One month," I said.

He put a small chunk of clay on the mother's abdomen and smoothed it over. "Now say two months."

"Two months," I said.

He put another chunk of clay on and smoothed it.

"Now three months."

"Three months!" And more clay.

By the time we got to nine months the lady was monstrous. "She got big in front and on her sides, too." And presently, "Now the baby's going to come. I'll be the doctor this time and," offhandedly, "you can be the nurse. Take her to the hospital, father. Here she is. Out comes the baby. Hm. What do you know? It's another boy. See, you people. You've got two boys. One's three and the other's just a baby. You can go home in a few days. But I want you to be careful. That's

117

enough babies for a while. Remember now to do it just for love."

But after the mother arrived home where the big brother had been waiting, there transpired a curious turn of events.

Scowling fury stormed into Ken's face. "You should have known," addressing the mother, "it was much too soon to have another baby." And grimly wordless, he pounded a shower of bombs down on the baby until it was buried under the heap.

His intent came out even more clearly in the following session. He went through the baby scene again and at the end he exclaimed, "We'll bomb the father for asking the mother to have another baby. They already have one. That's enough. Brothers are nuisances. They're bad." And, turning to the father, he shook a warning finger at him. "Next time, you're not to have a baby brother. Next time you do it just for love."

EIGHTEEN

We had babies until the census bureau would have been astonished at the accelerated rate of population increase had not Ken as big brother demolished them as fast as they were born. However, a day came when Kenneth stepped into quite another role.

From the cupboard he fetched the syringe with the rubber bulb at the end of it. "See," he announced, "this is my thing. This is *my* thing to shoot baby seeds with." He filled it with water and sprayed it. "They're *my* baby seeds I'm shooting. I'm shooting my baby seeds like any old man."

Presently he stopped short for no open reason and sheepishly returned the syringe to its shelf. In the following session he made no allusion to what he had done. He went back to

119

being the big brother. In that one brief moment, however, he had been the big man. *His* thing had shot baby seeds.

Looking back later I could see this day standing like a sign post. It pointed in the direction which he was to travel for many long months.

What we had done was by no means finished business to be catalogued and laid aside till adulthood arrived. *The facts of life* could not be real or valid to Kenneth until he had made them into what he could label *My Facts of Life*. As impersonal facts they were relatively unimportant. Their significance lay in what they had to do with him and in what he had to do with them.

Cathy had told Kenneth where babies came from and that when he grew up he would have babies of his own. She had conscientiously, with the help of good books at her elbow, imparted the facts. But, like many another parent, Cathy would have been surprised that even though Ken had appeared to absorb this information as it was given him, now, such a little while later, he sounded as if he had absorbed not a thing. Actually the facts parents give as explanation are only fill-ins or clarifiers. And they cannot clarify properly unless they take into account what the child's thoughts are. To him the realest part of the picture comes, for one thing, from what he sees and hears and feels around him and, even more, from what he makes of this in his mind. He gets cues openly or subtly from what his parents mean to each other. He ties these in with the sensations of his own body. His impressions spread their wings in fantasy and mate in flight with wishes that he often feels should-not-be and with guilt and anxiety. And these in turn let misshapen offspring wing their way into adulthood to destroy the richness of mating and loving and creation and birth.

A child may have the picture straight enough when it's about *a* man and *a* woman, *the* father or *the* mother. He may even manage to keep it straight when it's about his father and mother. But when he begins to get the image of himself as father or mother, then the facts become vague in a mist of fear.

I had listened in on many of Ken's fantasies and now in our baby scenes I had helped him sift out some of the facts. He had gradually made his wonderings apparent. Already in the accretions of clay on the fertile mountain, he had, for instance, confessed his wonderings about a mother's fertile belly; in the Easter eggs with cracks and wee-wee holes, his concern with the mother's cracks and holes; in his play with syringes and snakes, his fantasies about the father and his role. Many things that he had confused were now clearer. Many disparate elements were now integrated into this one story of birth.

Kenneth now knew how babies were conceived and born. But he still had ahead of him a far bigger and more disturbing question: *How does this apply to me?*

Parts of his inner-made answers had flashed now and again across the sheet of his vision. But just as swiftly he had jerked these back out of sight. He would need to bring more of his fantasies into view more distinctly before I could know enough of his feelings to help him understand the realities and how these coincided or conflicted with *his* realities—*his* facts of life. I would need to listen and watch.

Again he went about poking into holes and wetting into them. Only the wet, now, he often called "baby seeds" and it went more often frankly into the mother's baby hole.

As long as the thing remained impersonal all was simple

and clear. But soon from deep in his mind the question of identities wriggled in its chrysalis and tried to push its way out. Who was he? And who was the mother? And what was he imagining himself doing? And where?

He had a dream. Four people lived in a house: a father and a mother and a good boy and a bad boy. And the father and the bad boy went away and the mother and the good boy stayed home together.

It was a simple dream. But when he started to play it out with puppets, something went wrong. "The good boy stays home with his mother in her house and he does things for her like her husband used to do before he went away. He takes the hose and waters her best flower pot." He put his hand to his forehead. "I've got a headache. I don't want to play this game any more."

He had another dream: He was walking in the forest and he came to a funny little house, kind of an Eskimo hut. And there was a fire in it and it was cozy and warm. And the mother whose house it was said he could sit down near the fire. He did. And she sat down beside him and nobody else was there, just he and the mother, like husband and wife! And he rocked back and forth and the whole house rocked with him, like a rocking chair, sort of. And he felt warm and good. Only then the lady suddenly turned into a horrible monster and told him he was bad and started to gobble him up.

He told a story. Again he came to a house where a nice mother lived. And he reached out his hand and opened the door and walked in. He was going to be the "onliest boy there"—again like a husband, the important male. Only then the nice mother turned into a mean old witch and put him out, and the only way he could go back in and get anything to eat was by dying and being a ghost instead of a boy.

This theme he repeated many times. He wanted to be the "onliest" with the mother and go into her house as if he were her husband. But there was always disaster lurking and always there eventuated some harm.

When dreams such as these brought peeks into his unconscious, they frightened him and he would, almost as if in a panic, move into scenes of disaster. He would slice and shave clay snakes to nothing. He would cut off arms and amputate legs. It was obvious by now that the destruction of snakes and legs and arms were like "token" destructions, as if, by destroying substitute objects, the most important object might be saved. And more and more often this followed as punishment for wanting to have the mother all to himself.

But his discontent with this state would soon become apparent. He would paint trees with great branches stretching. And he would roll out bigger and bigger snakes. Then the snakes would start crawling into holes. And the trees' branches would poke into clouds and out he would bring the "squirter" and squirt into any hole or hollow he could find.

On the heels of this would come another dream about a boy wanting to be his mother's husband. But herein lay the danger. Again it would drive him back into slicing or destroying once more.

He invented a game that contained the whole cycle of wanting to be male, of feeling that such "badness" necessitated destruction, and of seeking nonetheless for some way to achieve it.

He made a clumsy clay figure and called it a "monster boy." He laughed gleefully. "See, he's got a nose and tiny eyes. And a huge penis, just enormous. It looks like an enormous cigar."

Then he made rings of clay and threw them around the

monster boy's organ, "Like a game where you throw horse-shoes over a peg. Or rings over a stick . . .

"Now it's the lady's turn. She throws the ring. And the monster boy laughs, 'Ho, ho! Come on, mother, get your ring around me!' " Again there had been that telling slip of the tongue.

"But he mustn't do that. He's very bad. He deserves to be punished. We'll have to pull parts of him off."

This he did. He amputated the arms entirely and the legs partially till they were "little stumpy legs, just big enough to waddle with." And then he went for the head. "Mr. Monster," he said, "your head deserves to be punished, a head that doesn't know any better than to have that big cigar sticking out right in front where the mother's ring can go around it. Shame on you! Put it down, do you hear me? Push it down between your legs like a tail. Hide it or it might get hurt."

He sat studying the situation till he had another thought. "I know," he said to the monster. "You're hungry." And to me, "He eats more than a pig and he 'specially likes fish. His father has a fish for him, fortunately. A great big one. He pops it into the monster boy's mouth."

He took a chunk of clay and pretended to put it into the monster boy's mouth. "And now see what happens? It makes him grow bigger!" And Ken molded clay onto the monster boy's stomach as he had done earlier on the pregnant mother's.

I thought of how sometimes unsophisticated adolescents believe that a kiss will beget a baby. And how often younger children fantasy that babies are started through the mouth.

Was Kenneth now resurrecting such fantasies from his younger days? At least through eating father's fish he was repeating what he had done earlier in therapy. He was taking something from father to nourish him and magically give him a secret inner growing strength.

"See," he pointed to the monster, "his stomach is big now and I made his little warty nipples big too. He's got a huge fish in his stomach. It turns into big jobs. No, into a baby. Or into a penis. A baby's a penis. You silly thing. He ate a fish and he got a baby. He has a penis-baby inside him, sticking way out in front!"

He was obviously returning once more to a solution he'd had before: be a girl. But, as if to offset danger, he was creating a world in which a girl was no penis-less creature. Every hollow contained a protuberance. In the hollow between this monster's legs lay the big cigar thing. And in the belly lay the baby that made this creature stick out in front. Or, if Kenneth desired, the thing inside her might become brown penis big jobs that could be indefinitely reproduced. Thus, in the world of his own creation this monster man-woman had not lost what he'd fantasied his mother had lost for being bad. While the thing that had set this into action was the mother's ring around the big cigar.

I watched the monster boy waddling and Kenneth grinning a silly, evasive kind of grin. "If he keeps his big fish-penis in his stomach," I put in, "it won't get knocked off. But the big cigar-penis might if it stopped hiding and stuck out in front and got the lady's ring around it."

He sat back on his haunches and eyed me in wonderment. "My goodness, Dorothy. How did you know?"

Except for the allusion to father's fish, Kenneth these days was conspicuously leaving father out. Just so, in the months that passed, did Cathy leave Vic out; and Vic Cathy. The breach was becoming more apparent though it was not new.

It had actually been present since the beginning of their marriage, as Vic had mentioned the very first time he'd talked with me when he had spoken of his feeling that he and Cathy had really never been close.

To Cathy the thought crawled gradually and insidiously into focus: Vic had said nice things to Loretta in that note. He didn't draw into himself with Loretta. He didn't run away from her. Thank goodness Loretta hadn't stayed in this part of the country. Thank goodness she had gone back to join Jim. But somehow this wasn't reassuring enough. Cathy had to do something more about it. She could not hold herself in check.

"See, Vic, I bought myself a new negligee. I hope you like me in it."

"Yes, Cathy, I do!"

But for Cathy this still wasn't enough. If she were Loretta, Vic would say more. "Vic!" she pleaded. "Doesn't it make me look . . . well," she smiled in apology and turned her face from him, "well, more sexy?"

He sat there in the big upholstered armchair, his long legs bent, his great feet angling out. His hands sprawled on the chair arms, limp and helpless. He didn't know what to say.

"It's all right, Cathy. Yes, it's all right."

Poor Vic! The thought flashed through her. He was so pathetically inexpressive. Maybe he had been this way with Loretta, too, in her presence. Had he? She wondered. Or was he this way only with her?

Vic's focus slipped silently away from Cathy. He'd had a note that day from Loretta. She'd broken off with Jim. She wanted Vic to be the first one to know.

Vic sighed. His mind's eye caught sight of a golden straw in the dung-heap: Perhaps soon Loretta would be back in town!

NINETEEN

Kenneth was nine now. Leaner. Longer boned. Straighter. A straighter look in his eyes. He'd been in therapy with me for a year-and-a-half. His asthma was much improved. He would go for two weeks, three weeks, occasionally for a month without it and when it did come, the attacks were far less severe.

When he finished the first half of his fourth grade, his principal telephoned me. "Hello," she said, "and Hallelujah!" with dignity flown to the winds. "About our boy, Kenneth. I was right. He's come out with all A's. And what do you think? On his Achievement tests, his reading level is *eighth grade*. Imagine that for a fourth grader! And *that's* the boy whom *they*," with a snort, "labelled 'dumb.'

"He's still on the retiring side in his dealings with the other youngsters. But he's coming along. At least he eats lunch with them now outside on the playground instead of creeping off alone into a corner of the classroom. As for his I.Q., we haven't given any individual tests this year. How about your giving him one in your office?"

I thought we'd wait a while longer till he had come out of his shell still further and could use every bit of that fine gray matter under the blond shock of hair.

I was hopeful and triumphant. But my triumph was destined to be short-lived. There was trouble ahead.

Vic lost his job.

Mr. Taylor, his boss, had been ailing. He came to the office with face white and pinched. Vic was devotedly on hand to carry out his last bidding. "What would you like done about the Brody job, Mr. Taylor? I'll be glad to do it for you if you let me know what you want" . . . "Yes, surely, Mr. Taylor. I'll write up that Damascus report. What would you like me to say?" . . . "The Plunkett stuff isn't working out too well. I didn't want to take it on myself to settle it. What do you think should be done?"

Mr. Taylor regarded him with vague, half-seeing eyes and let his questions slide by half-answered. But one day, with the pinched puckering about his colorless mouth more ridged than ever, Mr. Taylor told Vic that Blaine Ross was taking over management of the firm.

Blaine Ross arrived. Cathy was asked with Vic to the cocktail party that Mr. Taylor gave to introduce Blaine to employees, associates and clients.

Cathy looked curiously at Blaine. She saw dark gray hair aging from intense blackness, gray eyes with black pin-point sharpness and hands that in their vigorous gesturing seemed more like fists. They were hard hitting hands and betrayed a hard hittingness in the man. Brutal hands, Cathy thought. In a swift inner vision, she saw Blaine's face darkening in temper and for some strange reason a small chill went down her back.

Blaine Ross was eager, open, aggressive. Cathy's mind hung in space with the word and then clicked: Aggressive. That's it. The very thing that Vic isn't.

All at once Cathy knew that she had been pinning a pale little patch of threadbare hope over the anxiety that showed naked beneath: Blaine Ross had the position she'd wanted Vic to get. The position that Vic would have had if Vic had been more aggressive. Vic knew enough about the firm, about the jobs, about Mr. Taylor's policies and his manner of handling the business. To Vic had fallen the lot of understudy to Mr. Taylor. As for his thorough-going knowledge of structural engineering, there was no question about that. Even today he was planning to stay till the guests thinned out to take up some confidential last minute details on a job that was pending. Vic knew his stuff. Blaine was no smarter. In fact, as Cathy listened to Blaine she felt he was not as smart. But much more aggressive.

Blaine's erect back, his direct look, his hard-punching gestures, these hurt her in their contrast to Vic's stoop and the backward pull of him. Stop it, Cathy, she told herself. Stop thinking such thoughts. But the thoughts rose to the surface in spite of her attempts to push them down.

When the crowd thinned, Vic went into the library with Mr. Taylor and Blaine turned to Cathy. Would she have a last drink?

His hand was steering her into the sunroom where the bar was set up. It was no longer hard and fist-like. It cradled her elbow. His voice was strangely confiding after such short acquaintance. He was looking for a place to live, he told her. Just a bachelor apartment. He didn't need a house since he'd been divorced a short while back and his boys were with his wife in the small town where they'd lived in upstate New York.

So he had boys, too?

He pulled out his wallet and flipped over the cellophane envelopes with his driver's license, his Masonic card, his Rotary membership, American Legion . . . until he came to the photograph of his two boys and their mother. "I don't have a picture yet of the boys without her," he explained.

The older boy was blond and serious. The way Kenneth would look in four or five years. And the woman wore a drawn expression, as if she were in pain. Cathy thought: as if he had beaten her! And again that strange shiver ran along her spine.

Blaine turned to her. "It's good to talk to someone, Cathy." He smiled down at her, his dark eyes lighting, and he reached an arm around her shoulder and gave her a genial hug. "I'll be calling you and we'll talk again."

To Cathy it was as if the sun had burst from behind fog. "The day was suddenly filled with color, no longer gray."

All these things Cathy had told me and in the next weeks the wish inside her kept rising into one perpetual question: Will Blaine call me?

Blaine did not call Cathy. But he called Vic into his private office, and from behind Mr. Taylor's great mahogany desk, he told Vic that he was reorganizing the business and for the time being would not need Vic's services.

Vic said, "That's all right." Nothing more. Next day, however, he went back and doggedly questioned, "What's wrong, Blaine? Why are you letting me out? It's important for me to know."

Blaine had said there was nothing against Vic. Only right now he needed men of a different type, more aggressive. "You're the research type, Vic; the inventor, the investigator. Right now that's not what this place needs. We need people who can promote. Push. Why don't you open a consulting service? When we come up with a tough problem we'll use you. It's a deal. But at present we don't need your kind of a man here full time."

That night there was a group psychotherapy session. Cathy came in, the air of a crusader about her, her dark head high. Vic followed, dragging his feet.

Glancing around the already gathered circle, Cathy chose the straight-backed chair from the two that were still empty and Vic, looking helpless, sank into the low armchair and huddled over himself.

The hum of greetings between the group members stopped as the doctor glanced at his watch. "Well," he said, swiftly surveying each face in the circle, "it's time for us to get to work."

There was silence and a few moments of waiting for some group member to spontaneously start to talk about whatever lay on his mind. For into this warm, big room with the quiet of shadows on the wall and the circle of waiting faces, these people once a week brought their troubles and feelings and fantasies just as Kenneth brought his into the room where he played. Here, the doctor and I, as joint psychotherapists, had

131

come to stand as a new father and mother. Under our guidance, these men and women with their diverse problems had grown to speak as freely as they would alone.

Tonight it was Cathy, not Vic, who began.

"It isn't fair," she protested. "It shouldn't have happened to Vic!"

She went on to recount what Vic had told her. She was angry, she said, at Mr. Taylor for not having protected Vic. "After all the years that Vic's been there. Why, he's been Mr. Taylor's right hand man. I think it's a darn rotten deal. Especially being told he's not the aggressive type!"

Cathy's voice was patiently sweet with martyred indignation. "That's like a slap in the face! What if Vic isn't the aggressive type? Vic's got a lot of other qualities . . ."

With quick perspicacity, several group members picked up Cathy's feelings. They now came out with thoughts that people ordinarily keep unsaid.

This is part of group psychotherapy. For when a person sees in the group how others react to him with the covers of pretense shorn off, he can at one and the same time see how he affects people outside the group. How he reacts in turn with hurt or anger, with impotence or with gestures of appeasement, stands out in clean silhouette. He can see more clearly what he is and how he is and what there is in him that upsets others and brings trouble onto himself. In the circle of the group he experiences safely and without harm in microcosm the undercover reactions which in the macrocosmic circle of his life outside the group bring him trouble.

With perceptiveness reaching with honesty toward honesty, one group member now hit on the falseness in Cathy's exaggerated sympathy.

"Come on off your pedestal, Cathy."

And another, "You're damned mad at Vic for not being more aggressive and you know it."

"I'm not." Cathy sat straighter and stared around the circle of faces, her hands trembling. "I'm not mad at Vic. Why should I be? I feel sorry for him. I'm mad at that damned Taylor."

"How do you feel, Vic?" another group member asked.

"I *don't* feel, I guess. That's still the trouble. I don't think it matters too much, if you know what I mean. I think Blaine's suggestion about my opening a consulting office is a good one and that's what I'm planning to do, and some of the clients I've worked with will come to me, I'm sure, as soon as they know I'm on my own. I think Blaine himself will use me, and I'll do all right. I'm not really worried."

This time the group reacted to his feelings. Some were friendly, some were challenging, some were frankly angry at him for the absence of vigor in his response. He persisted passively, "It doesn't bother me!" He showed no anger at their anger. No backfiring to their challenges. No appreciation, either, for the friendly concern.

Finally the doctor pointed out, "You have the same problem here, don't you, Vic, that you had on the job? You take all the criticism here without protest. You don't work up any aggressiveness. Let's see, now, how does it really make you feel when the rest of the group jumps all over you?"

Vic looked at the floor and swallowed. He uncrossed his long legs and recrossed them. "It doesn't matter, if you know what I mean."

"What do you mean, Vic?"

He swallowed again and turned toward Cathy, his great hands hanging limply over the arms of his chair. "It doesn't matter," he said and added without change in pace or pitch,

133

"It doesn't matter as long as Cathy thinks I'm all right."

The response rose quickly from various people.

"You sound like a little boy feeling fine as long as his mama says he's O.K. Just like me."

"As long as mother thinks you're wonderful, you don't have to struggle. The world can go by."

Vic's eyes were narrowed like blue slits of water almost lost in their hollows a great distance off. "My mother did think I was wonderful. My mother and Cathy."

His voice did not as usual plod on in monotone to indecisive end without ending. It paused in distinct waiting as if for something to rise from inside him rather than to come from the group.

"My father was away a lot, travelling for a firm he worked for. When he was at home, he was cold and aloof and disapproving of everything I did. I never felt close to him. I'd try to do things to please him when he was around, like getting his slippers for him or kissing him goodnight because he expected it of me, but I'd kiss him gingerly and notice how sharp his whiskers were, like barbed wires telling me to stay on my own side of the fence and not to get in his way or his territory or something, if you know what I mean. I tried to do things to please him, but it never did any good. He'd pack up and leave. I never really had a father. We never were close. I took Mr. Taylor as a father, I guess. I looked up to him and admired him and felt close to him and showed him I was there to do whatever he said. I guess that's got something to do with it, my always doing what he said. If I'd shown more initiative I might be managing the firm now. But I always looked to Mr. Taylor as the one who held the reins. He was so much older . . ."

"The man with the whiskers!"

"Well, I took him that way. As a father."

"And now the only father you ever had walks out and leaves you. But it doesn't really matter, you say, because you have Cathy. I used to say my father could walk out and go to hell and I wouldn't care. But I've seen recently that it mattered a hell of a lot. I was just covering up that I cared, so that the caring wouldn't hurt quite so much."

The doctor came in again. "You thought it didn't matter then, Vic, because you had Mother. You tell yourself it doesn't matter now because you have Cathy."

Vic nodded slowly. "Mother and I were close. But somehow I guess it did matter. I had to be man of the house, if you know what I mean . . ."

"What, Vic?" I asked.

"Well, I did things for Mother. Took care of the furnace and chopped wood and shovelled snow and other things, too, that were more just for her. Just between the two of us, if you know what I mean." He looked for all the world like a frightened overgrown boy who wanted to slink out and hide in some dark retreat with his guilty but cherished secret.

"What, Vic? What sort of things?" I hoped he could share with me now the secret things he'd shared with his mother earlier, only now show them openly in front of these other people, discovering as he did so that in reality he had nothing to fear.

"Well," he swallowed and cleared his throat, "things like brushing her hair. She had blond hair, long and like silk. When she had it unbraided it came to below her waist. She'd let me unbraid it. And I'd run my fingers through its length, straightening it all the way . . ." Vic's eyes were now very blue, focused as if off into distance. "She had a white ivory hair brush with a woman's figure carved on the back. Only a hole had been burned into the girl someway by a branding iron. That's silly, by a cigar or cigarette, I don't remember. And I forget where the hole was in her, what part of her was missing, just that there was a hole somewhere. I'd like to brush her hair; it felt soft and good and there were other things, too, like that, if you know what I mean."

"That felt good?"

He nodded.

"Well," he looked down at the floor. "Well, she'd like me to sleep in bed with her when *he* was away, and I'd wash her back for her when she bathed. She liked me to do it, take care of her, sort of . . ."

"She thought you were wonderful, Vic," the doctor said gently. "How did you feel, Vic? Protected and safe?"

Vic's eyes almost closed till the blue scarcely showed. He looked down at the floor away from everybody, as if he were afraid to meet anyone squarely. Then, in a voice that was duller and flatter and yet tighter and less flaccid, he answered, "No. Not safe really. No. I didn't really feel safe with my mother. I don't understand it. There was something about it. Well, it seems to me somehow . . . It came to me just at this moment . . . I never thought so before, but . . . Well, as if she had in some way expected too much."

"Like Cathy now?"

He scuffed his great feet on the floor in a helpless gesture, and very slowly shook his head.

TWENTY

Cathy was dejected, tired. Her head ached. As she told me about herself, every other word was "Poor Vic."

She was helping him get his office set up. She was helping him line up a list of potential clients. "Poor Vic, he's so worried. We're getting low on cash. I wish he could work up more enthusiasm. He just can't seem to get himself started. But then, that's only natural after the raw deal he got."

One thing both of them felt strongly. They did not want to stop therapy. They felt they needed it more than ever. To help pay for it as well as to help in the support of the family, Cathy found a part-time job in a circulating library in her neighborhood. And we cut the therapy fees so that they could fit them into their budget.

One day, after finishing her job, Cathy went to the Taylor office to pick up some things Vic had left there and she ran into Blaine.

"Hello, Cathy. How's Vic doing?"

"All right, Mr. Ross."

"Mr. Ross? What's the idea? How about going across the street for a cup of coffee? You're not looking up to snuff."

She ran her hand across her forehead and shoved back her hair. "I can't, Blaine."

He made an impatient gesture and the thought rushed through her: he's going to hit me. She stood rooted, the small curling current shivering down her spine. She had an impulse to turn and run and was surprised when her voice sounded smooth and calm. "I'm sorry, Blaine. I've promised Vic to help him fix up his office."

"We'll make it another time, then. Soon, Cathy. I'll call you. I haven't forgotten. I've just been punch-drunk with work."

Vic maintained in the group that he was doing all right. "I'm taking it slowly. It seems better that way. Cathy wants to move faster than I do. We have different paces. She's wonderful, though."

He had a dream. He saw Loretta and looked into her eyes. There was a river in them, wide and calm. "I was in the river. It felt warm and good." . . . He thought of a swimming hole to which he'd gone as a child, sometimes alone, sometimes with other boys, but rather alone. When he was alone there were no comparisons. It didn't matter who swam fastest, who could dive from the highest rock, who had the broadest shoulders or the largest parts to boast about. He remembered his father's. They looked enormous as his father stood in the bathroom on one of his visits home, naked, shaving with a straight bladed razor and stropping it till it rang keen and sharp. The river was peaceful and warm, the bees droning in the heat hummed him into protected aloneness. The warm water around him rested his flesh. These things came to him when he thought of the dream of gazing into Loretta's eyes. More than anything in the world he wanted peace.

"That's like the dream I had when I felt things were too tough. Wanting to go back to mother's womb," a group member ventured. "Or at least into her lap!"

But Vic could not see it. Things weren't too tough. They were moving along as well as he could expect.

"How about Loretta?" another asked.

She was coming to town, planning to stay for a while. He and Cathy were both looking forward to seeing her.

"How about it, Cathy?"

She looked at Vic and smiled a sad smile of forgiveness. The space between them seemed filled with suspended calm.

That Kenneth felt the undercurrent of their tensions was clear, as was also the fact that he wanted to get angry and, for some reason, could not. It was all mixed up, too, as became apparent, with his trying to work out *his* facts of life.

He dreamed of going to a picnic ground. He looked around there for something to eat. But in vain. All the tables were empty. There was no food. Then he noticed a policeman who said there'd been a fight.

When I asked Ken what he thought of the dream, his answer came quickly. "The mother was too busy fighting with the father to feed the children."

He told a story about a boy who had a big wish inside him. He went to bed at night with the wish; he woke up in the morning with the wish. It was a secret wish but it finally came out. His father and mother didn't like each other's faces; their mouths turned down so much. So the boy kept wishing and wishing that their mouths would turn up. Then his would be able to turn up too.

It became more apparent that Kenneth had not only felt rejected as a hungry baby or child afraid that his mother would not feed him. He had also felt his mother's rejection of him as a male. And as a male he lived in constant fear of being hurt. Again and again this theme appeared in his play.

He kept making clay figures which were obviously replicas of himself. "He's an unhappy boy," he confessed one day. "Poor thing! He wants to be happy. He keeps wondering how. He's a cockeyed kid. See him? See him; how ugly? Mothers don't like ugly boys."

He went into his recurrent theme: "Booms! There he trips. His head is almost off. His arms are almost off. His legs are almost off and one of them got much too short."

And then came a fantasied solution that paralleled what he was doing in real life. "Poor boy! He has to go to bed now and stay there and his mother *has* to feed him at least once every day. He's happy at last. His worries are gone."

By being hurt and sick he could get his mother in ways not possible for a healthy boy. He coughed and wheezed every night and sometimes in the day. The attacks would yield fairly well to the medicine his mother gave him. They were not alarming; yet they kept recurring. Along with them he retreated into a semblance of his old tightness. His paintings were pallid. He called them "pretty." They were watered down and lacked the verve and the branching out quality that he had been putting into them.

As for any direct resentment to his father or mother, it would not come. He found it hard even to fight with his

140

brother. He hung back in his old way of a year and a half ago. He complained whiningly, without any fight in him. "Brad took my comic books" . . . "Brad's a nuisance. He's acting so silly and naughty these days. He's a regular pest." . . . "Brad took a nickel out of my pocket . . ." But complaining was as far as he could go. The push had gone out of him; the aggression was blocked.

The school principal called. "What on earth has happened to our boy? He's shrunk back into himself. And his work's slipping. He failed in spelling. When he reads, he trips over words that he knows very well."

It was as if Kenneth were holding himself tightly constricted, huddled into an armed truce with himself. This was like the false armistice between Cathy and Vic.

I tried to help him bring out the resentment I knew must lie underneath. One day, for instance, I picked up the puppets representing a father and mother and two boys. "They're having a bad time," I said. "Their mouths all turn down like the father's and mother's in your story." I suggested we have a puppet play. He shoved the smaller boy aside. "We don't need this one!" He then made the father and the larger boy play they were robbers—partners. They went together into a cave after some money. Each, however, then began to want the money for himself. "The one who gets it will take it home to the mother or the wife, I don't know which!" So they fought a great fight, and because the big robber was weak even though he was bigger, the younger robber killed him.

For a moment, Kenneth seemed almost gay. The tightness in his breathing started to let up. Then the smile faded and the tightness returned. The young robber was pursued by a policeman and got into an accident and was hurt.

Here Ken's voice dropped to a whisper. "Poor thing," he

said softly. "Poor thing was an orphan!" In this single bit of news, he told himself that what he had said earlier held no truth. The boy had no parents. He had won the battle, yes. But there was no mother to go home to. No confusion to deal with between mother and wife.

"Poor thing! He had no parents. That's how he got so bad. Nobody loved him when he was a little boy."

But dogs were loved.

"Hamburger had a girl dog come to see him. And he sniffed and sniffed and jumped up on her and stuck his penis in her baby hole, I think. I think it was the mother dog's baby hole, but maybe it was her big job hole. I couldn't see too well which it was. I don't think Hamburger was too sure either. He tried to investigate when he sniffed to see which it was. But she wouldn't let him find out.

"Hamburger got all excited," he declared. Kenneth's own excitement was apparent.

"And so did you?"

He nodded and laughed.

"And," more excitedly, "they made noises, snorting and sniffing . . ." He stopped short.

Suddenly worried, he questioned, "Tell me, Dorothy, why do they cut dogs' tails off?" The idea of excitement—his own excitement, not only Hamburger's—had brought the idea of injury in its wake.

To the following session he came in very tight, the wheezing perceptible.

"Did you know, Dorothy, that mother fish eat up their babies?" He was obviously frightened.

For all the bigness of him, he wanted to come on my lap. Once there, he seemed to feel safer and went on in a louder voice. "Yes, mother guppies eat their babies. I don't know anything you can do to stop them. The babies run away and try to hide in the plants. They stay very quiet as if they were dead.

"And yesterday, do you know what happened? My mother was cleaning the tank and she caught a baby guppy in the tube of the cleaner."

The anger had crawled up into his voice and the wheeze had vanished. "She should have been more careful. It was a boy guppy, too."

And then suddenly despair overtook indignation. "Why don't mothers want their babies to swim around and live?"

Later on the same day I saw his mother. As was usual these days, she came in filled with concern over Vic. She was full of sympathetic understanding. "Poor Vic! He got so tired. I've been doing whatever I can to help him."

She told me then that as she had been drifting into sleep two nights before, she had seen in the eyes of her mind a woman screaming in fury, attacking a man, trying to get his male organ into her mouth to bite and destroy.

Into my mind flashed what Kenneth had told me about the mother fish eating the boy baby. On one night, Cathy's unconscious feelings had risen in the dream of destroying. The next day Kenneth had brought in his fantasy of being destroyed. Had Kenneth apprehended what lay in Cathy's unconscious before she, herself, perceived it? Had he gotten cues from her actions, as perhaps from some gesture or tensing as she cleaned out the fish tank? Or was the parallelism coincidental in two lives reacting to similar events in the same place and time?

I asked Cathy what the fantasy made her think of.

"Vic's father when Vic was young!" she began. "His father

143

left him," linking thought to thought. " He gave Vic nothing. My father gave me nothing either. Promises. Promises. Nothing more." The promise of a smile, of hands cushioning elbows, lifting her in laughing play above his head.

Then clenched fists and anger and a belt ripping off from around his waist swirling at her and an angry voice muttering angry words. "He gave me an elephant. He gave me a baby. What kind of a baby? A baby teddy bear and I called him Kenny. No, Teddy. Teddy was his baby. Kenny his baby. I wanted his baby. Only I lost it. The elephant, I mean."

And now all softness went from her voice. It came with the hardness of stone grinding against stone. "I hate him. I hate Blaine. I hate all men. Vic too. He doesn't give me anything. No money. No sex. Why did he have to lose his job? Why couldn't he be more aggressive? Why didn't he rip off his belt and slash Mr. Taylor for doing him dirt? I feel starved and hungry. I want to tear him to pieces. Grab him. Bite him like the woman did in my dream. Oh, God, I wish I'd never had children. It's too heavy. Too hard."

TWENTY-ONE

Kenneth had left his session with the idea of injury and hurt on his mind. Baby fish hiding in the water plants in their hopeless attempts to evade destruction. Dogs' tails being cut off.

That evening Kenneth stood in the kitchen listlessly leaning against the sink. When Cathy told me about it later she recalled her own vague discomfort at Ken's eyes wistfully following her as she went about getting dinner.

"What are you doing here, Ken?" she tossed him an off-hand question and added, "Run along and play your radio."

He stayed but she hardly noticed. She was too abstracted, too engulfed by inner feelings pressing to rise into thoughts.

The taste of tears was a choking fullness in her throat. She could breathe the tear taste through the back of her nose.

From the refrigerator she took the blue and white bowl with the crack running through it and the nicked platter with the meat loaf on it. "Dilapidation," she thought.

In the bowl, the macaroni from last night was stickily congealed. She hated the stuff all stuck together, nothing clear and distinct. All gummed up, like her life. She was stuck in her marriage with no alternative. Working at the bookshop. Keeping house. Two boys to care for. If it weren't for them, she might have got free.

She twisted the old gold band on her finger. Vic's mother's. How she hated it now.

The meat loaf looked old and gray. Why bother to warm it? Let well enough alone, she told herself. Let well enough alone, Cathy. It's cold. Why bother to get it warm?

She reached into the drawer and pulled out the carving knife. She'd slice it the way it was. Any old way.

And then? It wouldn't come clear when she told it. But she heard herself scream and she looked down and saw blood. The ring lost in blood.

She fainted.

When she came to, Kenneth was leaning over her, his face yellow-gray with terror, the freckles pale lavender scars. "Don't leave me, Mother. Please, please, Mother. Please don't die."

Just then Vic came in through the door.

That night Kenneth coughed and wheezed and struggled for breath. To Cathy he seemed to be strangling. "The way he used to all the time."

This was the worst attack of asthma he had had in the year

and nine months since I'd known him. In that time he had come to realize his need for food, warmth, comforting and appreciation and to glimpse his own anger over having been deprived of these values. He had also come to see that he needed acceptance not only as an individual but as a male individual. Moreover, the fear of rejection and the anger over it carried connotations also having to do with boy guppies being destroyed, dogs' tails being cut, his own tail being cut.

The sight of his mother's finger cut and bleeding had suddenly touched off all these dreads and had rekindled anger, as became apparent in what ensued. But the anger right now could not come out clearly. His mother's cutting her finger had thrown him back into too grave fear. So the asthma persisted, a physical expression of the emotional conflict going on within. For a week he wheezed violently day and night. All medication was of no avail. He could not eat; he could not sleep; he could not talk; he was too concerned with the tremendous and vital necessity of breathing. The doctor did what he could, administering everything possible to bring relief.

Finally at the end of a week of ineffectual medical treatment, since Kenneth could not come into the office, the doctor decided that I should go to his home to see him.

When I went into Kenneth's bedroom, he was sitting in bed, propping himself on the flat palms of his hands behind him, huddling forward, his chest heaving, his shoulders hunched up. His pupils were wide as in fear.

"You've had an awful time, Ken!" I said and went toward him and sat on the edge of his bed.

He smiled wanly at me and wheezed.

I sat for a little while quietly with him and then, knowing he couldn't, I started to talk. I told him I knew his mother had cut her finger and he'd seen her faint. Almost imperceptibly

147

he nodded. I wondered if the blood perhaps reminded him of things he'd played about, like the soldier's leg. He nodded again. I told him that I had a couple of guesses about some other things he might have been thinking, and it seemed to me his eyes asked: what?

"Her finger looked kind of like the dog's tail, didn't it? The way you'd been thinking of its being cut?" Again his nod. "And it made you afraid of lots of things. Of other things that might get hurt and cut? On you, maybe? Because of thoughts you've had and things you've done that you've imagined were bad."

The stiffness in his elbows suddenly let loose. He lay back and shut his eyes and neither of us said anything. And after a few minutes he put out his hand and touched me and whispered, "You have time for me, don't you? You won't send me away?"

"No," I said gently, feeling that he was fearing once more, as he had of old, that his anger might make his mother leave him since the possibility of her leaving had seemed so close in the possibility of her death. And now, he was transferring the possibility of loss onto me.

"You're afraid I might leave you, aren't you, Ken, because of those thoughts? So, out with them now. The sooner the better. Because you know we've noticed before this that when you don't own up to thoughts you're ashamed or afraid of, they're apt to come out in wheezes instead of in words!"

He said nothing and went on wheezing and I sat quietly by and waited. And then through the wheezing came a small-voiced complaint, of all things, about Hamburger's bark. "Hamburger barks all night." It disturbed him. He couldn't sleep.

"It bothers you terribly," I said, and waited again, knowing there must be more.

"Yes!" he struggled. "Hamburger barks outside the house in the night. Poor little dog. He doesn't sound happy." The words were coming more easily. "He's shut out and lonesome. He's neglected . . ."

He paused a moment, struggling for breath. "Can you understand dog language, Dorothy?"

"I used to think I could. Can't you understand what they say?"

He nodded. "I can sort of understand Hamburger. He was shut out and neglected." He paused a moment. And then, gathering strength, he announced, "He's *mad*. He's *furious*. When Hamburger's put to bed tonight he will want to get up and bite all the people who shut him out."

It was my turn to nod. "Dogs are just like people, aren't they?"

"Yes, just like people. *Mad*."

His wheezing, I saw, had let up noticeably. He lay back more relaxed and repeated, "Mad."

With this oblique acknowledgment of his own anger which he had had so much difficulty in expressing, his wheezing lessened. And then, unbelievably, he laughed.

"Dogs are so funny. They come in and they shove their funny black noses—the little, round wet tip of their noses—right in your ear. Just like people, they want to get in. They want to go in and shove the husbands and brothers out and be inside the mother and be the *onliest* one."

I nodded and said, "Just like a lot of children do, too. They want to be inside the mother and be the onliest one."

He looked reassured. "Yes, they do!"

"But," from me, positively, "they don't have to get their

tails cut off for that. And they don't have to get sent away."

"No, they don't." He sighed and took a deep breath.

The fear was somewhat allayed. The yearning was expressed! The anger had come into the open. And now the wheezing was gone.

In the morning, however, it started again. So Kenneth came to the office and we talked some more and played "Hamburger nose games."

"Hamburger wants to be the husband and shove out the real husband," he concluded near the end of the session. "He wants to get in and he feels neglected and shut out and unsatisfied. He goes sniffing and poking with his nose because he wants to get inside and see what's in there. And he's *mad* that he can't."

"Only," I said, "poor thing, he's been so scared to say he's mad that he's wheezed instead."

We both laughed to think of Hamburger wheezing.

"But," Ken said ruefully and without any sign of tightness, "he still wants to be the onliest one."

TWENTY-TWO

On the whole, Kenneth was having a hard time releasing his anger. That he was uncomfortable and resentful was evident. But he could not express it consistently. After the short spurt following his severe attack, he retreated. Days went by in which he could get nothing out. Neither could Cathy. As for Vic, "He's been so considerate," Cathy murmured, looking down at her bandaged finger. "He doesn't scold me for having been so terribly clumsy. He's been sweet to me. Well, as sweet as he can be when he's working so hard. He's dead by evening."

The brittle edge was showing through her smoothness. "He's . . . well, what I'd call the silent partner around the house. He doesn't communicate. He sits. He doesn't make love. He isn't sexy. He almost never comes near me, and when he does it's over so fast. I guess, though, no faster than it used to be, but somehow it seems so to me. As if he were trying to get it over with quickly. To get rid of me, to push me away. That's how it makes me feel. Beside which, it's been almost two weeks now since he's wanted me. He comes home, crawls in behind his paper; crawls into bed; goes to sleep."

Cathy stopped and bit her lip. "This isn't fair of me to talk like this. I've no right to complain. The whole thing is that Vic's dead tired. And no wonder; he's got so darn much to do. He's had to wash the dishes with the boys and help out in one way and another around the house since I hurt my finger. I've added this to the load he's carrying at the office."

She kept on berating herself, cutting herself figuratively into little pieces as she had cut her finger. What she was earning helped a little but she still felt so useless. She wasn't appreciative enough of all Vic was doing. She wasn't sympathetic enough of his struggle.

Again and again in the midst of it, she kept coming back to an old refrain. "I'm no good for the children."

She felt certain it was her fault that Ken had had more asthma since Vic lost his job. His bad attack this past week had been her fault. If she'd been able to take things more in stride without getting all tense and upset, Kenneth would not have been so upset either. She knew he reacted to her and her moods. She was convinced she should send him away. Find some good school. But how could she now? They couldn't afford it. She was just stuck.

Vic came into the group therapy session three nights after the peak of Kenneth's asthma attack, more stooped than ever.

He went to the most shadowed corner of the room and sat there in the circle of the group but as if he were isolated and inside himself chewing over his thoughts.

One of the group members brought in a picture he had painted at home crudely as a child paints, of a dream he had had. It showed three chickens. The mother hen in her steel gray feathers sat stony-faced not on a nest but on a block of granite. The father rooster stood opposite, solemnly regarding her. And on the ground between them lay a baby rooster, blood splattered over the whiteness of him, dripping from his abdomen and neck. The blood-flecked feathers scattered around him and the tell-tale splashes of blood on the father bore testimony that a struggle had gone before.

Vic stared at the picture as others began to react to it, telling what came into their minds as they looked.

"The hen might be a statue, a monument to chicken-motherhood. No more feeling in her than in my mother," one said.

"The little one tried to stand up to her and the mother wouldn't take it and slapped it down, and the father came along and finished the job. But the mother doesn't care. She's perfectly satisfied. She's thinking, 'You wouldn't do it my way, so that's what you deserved.'"

"The little chicken's menstruating . . ." said another.

Cathy leaned forward, her face taut. "Yes, there *is* blood between the legs." She was startled. "I didn't see it till this minute. I know what that is. That's what happened to me when I was a child. I saw what my brother had and I didn't have one. It must have bled like that when it was cut out. I hated my brother for having what I didn't have. That's why they liked him better than they liked me." Her fingers dug into the chair arms. "I wanted one like his or my father's. Then my father would have liked me better. I'd have belonged with him like my brother did, gone places with him, shared things. Why couldn't he have given me one?"

"Given you what, Cathy?" the doctor asked gently.

"A penis. A foetus. Feet. Fingers. He gave me my fingers. My hands are like his. So are Kenneth's, as if Kenneth were *his* child."

Cathy was staring at her bound finger. "Do you suppose I cut my finger instead of what I wanted to cut?"

"They told me they would cut mine off if I went on touching it. That's when my mother looked stoniest and my father got mad and thrashed me within an inch of my life."

Several brought in similar experiences and then a young dark eyed man said with a wistful dreaminess, "To me the picture means that the little chicken was trying to get into the nest with the mother." And with quick risen anger, "That's when the damned father bird killed it."

Vic's hunched shoulders straightened a little. He cleared his throat. "I don't know why it is, but that remark made me think. Or what was said before it did, I'm not sure which. But to my mind the little chicken wasn't doing anything.

"I used to get into bed with my mother and that didn't matter. I slept with her when my father was away, like I've told you before. That father has no reason to kill the small chicken. There's no gleam of reason in the father's eye. He's a stupid bird and he killed the small chicken out of stupidity. I've seen a good many small chickens get pecked up like that. Not because they get into bed with their mother or anything like that, but just because it's chicken nature, if you know what I mean. Or because the father's stupid. Or something."

Vic swallowed and slumped as if the effort had left him exhausted.

He said no more during the rest of the session. But the next day he called and asked to see me. Something had come into his mind, he said, after the group session when he'd gone to bed. Like a delayed take. It disturbed him. He wanted to talk with me about it and not wait till the group met again the following week.

As I hung up the telephone I thought: this is progress. Better than the impassivity and the winding sheet of calmness. Vic was at last owning up to feeling disturbed.

Vic sat down in my office and fumbled with the elastic band around the scroll he carried. He finally managed to twist it over the end and to uncurl the paper. He had written things out, he said, so that he shouldn't forget. He began to read.

"I remember at the age of perhaps four, mother told me that if I played with my tea-pot, it would fall off. I have no memory of the act, only the warning. As a clincher to her admonition, she cited the cases of the daughters of a neighboring family. They had lost their tea-pots for this very reason. And about this same time I saw one of these girls who was about my age squatting on the uppermost step of her porch. It was a bright sunny day. I was standing below on the ground thinking about what my mother had told me when the little girl started to wet. I can see the water running down over each successive step making a puddle in the dust at my feet. I think I must have compared this slipshod way of making water with my own as yet unaltered method . . . Nonetheless I continued to do what I was warned not to do." His hand dropped to his knees, the paper dangling while his voice plodded on. "I'd sneak the forbidden act in and finish it as quickly as possible, standing behind a tree or in the water closet or in back of the wood shed, or somewhere. But, I don't think I did it in bed . . . Maybe sometimes I did in my own bed . . ." He shook his head, puzzled. "Somehow, in bed seemed the worst. The hardest to hide or something. But anyway, every time I did it I was afraid the fateful day of losing my tea-pot would eventually dawn."

"It still makes you swallow in fear when you talk about it, like just now."

He nodded slowly. "I guess it does get me. Somehow it's helped make me uncertain with girls. That, and the fact that my parents never got along together. I never had any foundation in what it meant for a man to get along with a woman. I don't think my father ever had sex with my mother. She hated anything sexy or any man who was sexy. I had the impression that it was she who sent my father away, and that she sent him because he would sometimes try. Anyway, there was something about girls that scared me; something about being too sexy."

"Something about having feelings with a woman like those feelings you got when you touched your tea-pot?"

He looked at me seriously, his eyes very blue.

Whether Ken heard some whispering about Vic's disturbance as Vic took it to Cathy, I never knew. Perhaps Ken sensed more directly the feelings in his father and identified with the crippled self-portrait Vic painted of himself in his own mind. Perhaps Vic's fear for his tea-pot met with Ken's fear and in some way magnified it. These things were unclear. What was clear was that Kenneth had felt his mother's renewed wish to be rid of him and that his worry about his own body and the possibility of injury to it had increased when Cathy cut herself. The knife and the blood and the slashed finger had gone hurtling into his wish to be the "onliest" and

156

had hung spinning with his fantasies in the timeless appre
hension of danger preceding a crash.

Instead of daring to go on with his wish to be the *"onliest,"*
Kenneth retreated into being the *loneliest.* Whatever he felt
of Vic's panic might well have provided the additional ounce
that made the burden too heavy. There were days when he
wandered about aimlessly, counted squares on the brown linoleum tile, stood passively touching the pulleys on the blinds.
Nothing mattered.

At school he was failing in spelling. "I don't care." But his
tone was not rebellious. It was flat. His arithmetic papers
came back with half the answers miscalculated. He looked
blank and unconcerned. He wanted no Hamburger nose
games. He wanted no games at all. No play. No talk. He didn't
want anything. He couldn't even work up steam about Brad.
Brad took more of his comics, again broke his radio. But Ken
could only say blandly, "It's not his fault."

I asked, whose was it?

"Nobody's. Those things happen."

He wheezed on and off and looked weary and beaten. I
hoped life had not hit him so hard that he would not be able
to rally. He could not face all the problems at once. That was
certain. The danger he feared was too appalling. And the
anger that swept through him, as we gradually saw, was too
big.

When he started to paint again, in his retreat from ugliness
he made things pretty. Pale and pretty. They were not about
anything. "They're just pretty colors." He looked at me
blankly. "They're not really anything. Just pretty." I searched
for a belligerent note but could not find it. "They're just
nice," he avowed. "That's all."

"Like you're trying to be nice, Ken. Trying not to show anything that isn't nice?"

"About whom?" he asked cannily, at last showing the pinpoint of a spark.

"You think I want you to say things that aren't nice about certain people?"

"About my mother? But I think she's nice and pretty too. She helps my father." And with a far-away look, "She loves us sometimes, I think, but she doesn't have time to show it.

"And about Brad. He's just a silly flea or a monkey, hopping and chattering. He's irritating, but he doesn't really count."

"And about father?"

"He's big. And he's busy. I'm not mad at anybody."

He decided, however, to paint a "different picture." Of an airplane. "It's going to fly against the enemy."

It reminded me of those early days when through such play he had tried to build up enough courage to come out with feelings of anger and killing. Now again his thoughts were on killing. "It's a war plane, all right."

But he couldn't go on. "I've got to camouflage it. Now it looks like a peace plane. All camouflaged and pretty."

"Like you're trying to stay all pretty and camouflaged?"

"Why Dorothy!"

The exclamation was spoken as rebuke. The anger against me was kindling into more than a spark.

"You sound sort of mad at me, Ken."

"Yes," he said. "You guessed it. This time you're the good guesser!" derisively. "And," with rising frankness, "I don't like you. I don't like you at all."

I sat back, inwardly glad and hopeful. He said nothing further for the moment. But he mixed brown paint with more vigor and made brown bombs fall thick and fast from the camouflaged plane.

I laughed and asked if he might be trying to get the brown all over me. He laughed, too, and nodded. "They're big ones and they're stink bombs in case you don't know."

Then, as if this avowal had freed him, the wheezing lessened and he began painting out his own inner warfare against redness and blood. He painted animals with red legs. Monsters with gushing nose bleeds. Red snakes. Fish with red, running spots. He talked of having hurt himself, of having skinned his knee, broken off his finger nail, gashed his toe. There were new puppies up the block. Would their tails be cut? Would they bleed? How could the bleeding be stopped?

He dreamed that he and some other boys each owned a grasshopper. The other boys could make their grasshoppers jump up and down but he couldn't. His just stayed at the starting line and wouldn't hop up and down toward the finish. "It got hurt, I think, my grasshopper did. I think in my dream it was bleeding."

He couldn't sleep at night, he complained soon after.

"That's uncomfortable," I said. "Can't you do something to help you feel sleepy?"

"I count sheep."

"Which sheep?"

"Mary's little lamb-sheep, or Little Bo-Peep's . . ."

"Which?" I asked.

"The ones who left their tails behind them."

"What do you suppose happened to their tails?"

"Maybe they were cut off like those puppies' tails."

I nodded and then asked gently, "How about your tail, Ken? Are you giving all your attention to the sheeps' tails instead?"

"Oh, Dorothy!" There was a chuckle in his exclamation as well as a kind of invitation for me to go on.

I did. "Maybe way inside of you you want to pay attention to *your* tail instead of to theirs. Only you're afraid something might happen to it like happened to the puppies' tails. Or to Mother's finger?"

He looked at me very seriously. And after a few moments of looking, he said a curious thing. "Mother and Father might get mad. They whisper about it in their room. I hear them. They're working up madness. They don't want me to do it."

"And how do *you* feel then?"

He came back swiftly with positive and downright avowal, "I'm mad at them for interfering with my pleasure."

It was my turn to nod. "So how about that grasshopper?" I asked him. "The one that couldn't hop in your dream?"

He grinned a wide grin.

"I think I'll let it hop tonight."

TWENTY-THREE

In his last session Kenneth had declared anger but he had not brought much of it out. He had wheezed on and off since and was wheezing when he came in the next time. He announced, however, that he had discovered that his grasshopper could hop. Could it burrow, too? Into the ground? "Do grasshoppers have holes there that belong to them for burrowing purposes?"

He had been at a miniature golf course in his neighborhood the day before. "We had fun! There was me and Brad and Gene. He's a boy in the neighborhood."

Ken broke off and drew his eyebrows together. "Brad got two holes in one. He's good! I hope he doesn't improve any more!"

161

Then Ken went back to thinking about holes. During the golf game he'd wondered what went on down in those holes. And in holes like Hamburger dug into in the ground or like Hamburger's nose went into inside a person's ear. What's inside? "What do you see if you go exploring?"

"It sounds as if you'd like to explore?"

He smiled secretively.

"How about an exploring game?" I suggested.

"Or an exploring picture."

"O.K."

He put the finger paint on thickly, a pinkish red-earth color. "Here I go!"

His index finger slithered up through the thick paint.

I made no comment but I noted that he was exploring up a hole and not down into one.

"This hole first. A smelly hole, this one. Like when your finger goes into the ear . . ."

"Or?"

"Or into the big job hole."

He wiggled his finger back and forth through the thickish paint in a small zig-zag path. "Up. Up. Up. Finger, finger, finger, finger.

"And now," he announced, "he goes into the other hole with his head." His own head made a butting kind of motion. "It's bigger and it's dark. But he crawls in." His whole hand and wrist and arm slid through the paint, making a pathway upward.

"Can he see anything?" I asked.

"Yes. *I* see all kinds of things. I go up a little way and I see a couple of balls. Bigger than anything. They start rolling at me. They want to push me out.

"And then I go a little farther and I see something that

looks like a fish. A great big one. And it wants me out.

"And I go a little farther and I meet a monkey. It wants to push me out, too. But *it* doesn't matter. It's a silly thing that makes a lot of chatter and doesn't really count.

"And I go a little farther and I come to the baby." His smile was of quiet depths. He did not move; just sat with his hand curved and relaxed on the center of the warm earth-pink.

But presently, as though opening his eyes from sleep into waking, he moved his hands in circular motion. "The baby starts moving and rolling around and wraps all around me and we roll around together like wrestling. You can hardly tell which is which."

"You and the baby seem to be one?"

"Uhuh, we are."

So, he was that baby. This much was clear, as was also the monkey. He had used practically the same words about his brother the session before. The fish was strangely reminiscent of father's great fish of which he had spoken from time to time. And the balls a bit further down than father's fish? One might hazard a guess.

His hand commenced rotating more quickly in an orgiastic gathering of speed. Faster and faster. He was breathing freely but hard as if in travail. And presently, "It's time now, baby, for you to get out."

His hand turned and shoved downward, inching its way.

"Unghh. Unghh. It's hard work," he groaned. "They push and pull me. Everybody's trying to get me out."

He came near the edge of the paper and there his hand began scrabbling back and forth, back and forth, scraping and pushing, until finally with clawing fingers spread wide, he shoved with a gigantic heave out over the edge, ripping the paper with his nails.

"I tore her to pieces, I did it so hard."

And with a great sigh of exhaustion, "There now! I'm out."

He sat back, still breathing freely but hard, gradually quieting. Tired and pensive he sat there until presently he murmured to himself, wonderingly, "About ten years ago I was in there . . ."

More quietness. And finally, wistful and uncertain, as if he were decrying hesitance on entering untrod country, "I'm not in there; I'm glad I'm out. I'm never going back in . . ." He left the finished sentence in mid-air as if it were unfinished and turned his eyes to meet mine.

To me he had shown the terrible struggle he'd had in the tortuous effort of birth. To me he was now showing the small, whispered protest against the more than half-wish to not-be, to repose, to return.

He needed to rest for a moment. But not for too long. Not for long enough to sink into regret and yearning for what was forever past. Not long enough to forget the small sparkle of forward wishing with which he'd commenced.

Could I help him hold to the glimpse he had had that the smaller wish was truly the bigger?

"Yes," I said, hoping he could sense that I knew with him, in the heritage of being human, the pull of giving up to that other wish that had been wrapping him in its promise of peace. "You're all through being in there with the whole of you. That's over, Ken. But you were just beginning with the wish to have a part of you do the exploring."

He stared at me, very sober. For a moment. Then he smiled and a chuckle escaped him. He nodded eagerly and confided, "A part of me, yes. And it won't be my hand."

TWENTY-FOUR

Kenneth had declared his wish. So did Cathy. More and more urgently. She was after Vic not to lie drowsily in bed in the morning, to get up earlier; to be more enterprising; to push harder at getting clients; "He's so unorganized and lacka-daisical. As leisurely as if our bread and butter weren't de-pendent on his selling himself to more people." He had gotten an assignment from Blaine Ross. "But that just fell into his lap." Several other people whom he had known while in Tay-lor's office had made tentative approaches. "Why don't you follow them up more energetically, Vic? For heaven's sake. You let them slide out from between your fingers. You could have done consulting on that Plunkett job if you'd only gone after it." . . . "I want some plants, Vic, for the garden." . . . "I want to turn in my old sewing machine and get a new one." . . . I want. I want. I want. The phrase cropped up recurrently throughout Cathy's sessions.

"What is it, Cathy, that you really want?"

"A man, obviously. Sex. A man. Marriage. A father for my children. Not a ghost."

She recalled the time long ago when her mother was in the hospital having her brother. "I was alone in the house with my father. Just father and me. He played with me then." Her voice softened into the dreaminess of yearning reminiscence. "He would throw me onto the bed and lift me high in the air, his hands under my elbows or in under my arms. He was big and I rode on his shoulders and he had a funny smell . . . I think of smoke and sweat. Of feet pulling out of shoes on a hot day. Of nuzzling my head into his groin as far up as my head could reach when he stood high above me. I remember his talking to me about *our* baby."

She stopped, uncomprehending. "Our baby? Of course. 'When mother comes home with our baby.' That's what he said. With '*our* baby.' " Very slowly. "I thought he meant mine and his." And with a sharp rush of anger, "Then *she* came home and brought *her* baby. Hers and his. And he said 'our baby' to her, not to me . . .

"I played with my doll. It was father's baby. Father's and mine."

Like every little girl she had wanted her father to give her a baby. Like many little girls she had intermingled with this wish the excitement of play with father, of touch and scent and big-man contact. The sense of being taken and lifted to heights where one lost power over oneself. Like most little girls she had found that wishes beyond her stretch were vis-

166

ioned but could not be reached. Like most little girls she grew afraid and angry as her fantasies ran on swift feet ahead of her to where she could not go. And so she had imagined other ways of being with father. She would be a boy. She was his partner. She went with him to business and into the bathroom. She wouldn't have to stay out if she were a boy. She could go in through the closed door marked "Gents" and play boy-man games. Since they were not girl-man games, nobody would object. And father would not turn, swirling in rage, and beat her unmercifully with his belt.

She wasn't a boy. She was a little girl. She grew, and her mother taught her how to embroider. She would sit on the green carpet footstool with an old-fashioned embroidery hoop in her hands, punching into the taut material with her little old grandmother's stiletto. Punch, punch, punch. Watching her mother through the bathroom door bathing her brother, crooning over him one moment, and the next moment glancing up and over at Cathy with a changed expression making her face harsh. Then again turning back to Buzz and to crooning soft little warm songs of love. This wasn't Cathy's mother. This was Buzzie's mother. Not the same mother. A nice mother. Not hard and cross. Even her hands were different. Washing Buzzie as he stood in three-year-chunkiness in the bathtub. Washing him all over as if there were no dirty, smelly places on Buzzie as there were on her. No places that you were supposed not to touch. No in-places. Only out-places. When she was a baby maybe she, too, had had those out-places like before she was operated . . . Those whirling machines. Shiny instruments, steel and silvered. Crucibles. Tanks, Whirling discs. The sweet, sick smell. When she was in the hospital. When mother was in the hospital. Having Ken.

No, having Buzz. When she, Cathy, was at home alone with Dad.

"I want. I want. I want a man. Not a ghost."

She rode along with Vic, one afternoon, to the Taylor office and sat in the car parked outside. Blaine came down with Vic to say "hello." How strange, she thought, the two together. Vic was taller. Blaine was stronger. Why couldn't Vic be like Blaine?

Blaine called her the next day. He hadn't forgotten. He'd been so busy. The business now, though, was picking up and he was getting around to treating himself to some of the things he'd been wanting to do. "How about cocktails?"

Cathy whispered to herself not to seem too eager after all the promises and the time that had been skipped. Softly, Cathy. Go slowly.

She made a date with Blaine for the following week.

It was then, as she hung up the telephone, the thought came to her: I'm through with mother. I don't want Vic with his soft hands like mother's hands bathing Buzz. His hands on me. I don't want Vic's hands. I want another part of his body. And he denies me.

"Give me plants, Vic, for the garden. Give me something. Give me sex."

"I'll try, Cathy. In the old way. I can't manage any other. You used to be satisfied. You thought it was your fault and that I wasn't happy with it. I told you that I didn't care. I wish you'd believed me and not gone into all this psychological business. What's it done? What's it doing? It's wrecking our lives."

"I hear them in their bedroom." Ken would lie tight and

rigid. His legs tight, his chest tight, his breathing tight in his body. "They're apart and leading their own lives in the same house. They speak to each other but they don't really talk.

"It's frightening.

"It doesn't feel good to a child this way . . ."

Angry hurt would well up in him. But he would shut back the tears, shut back the anger, shut back his wish to tear out of his room, pound on their door and shout in fury and rage. Even to me he still could not avow so big a wish.

"I toss and turn and I can't go to sleep. I want to hear and I don't want to hear . . . And when I fall asleep finally, I dream all the time.

"The real trouble is with their loving. That's where the real trouble is."

TWENTY-FIVE

To Vic it seemed there could be no peace with Cathy. He remembered his dream about Loretta. He turned his eyes from sleep and longing to Loretta herself.

The small bungalow she had found on the edge of a willowed ravine offered him shelter and rest. He would drop in at odd moments and sink into the chair in front of the fire. Through half-closed eyes he would watch Loretta on the floor beside him pouring coffee at the low table, offering him sugar and cream in the morning, a crisp salad at noon or a hot bowl of soup. Loretta ready with a highball toward evening. Offering him ready chatter, the anecdotes tumbling from her lips. Loretta offering the gayety of easy laughter. Offering him glimpses into the books of prints and reproductions she'd picked up during the summer abroad, offering him curious old photographs in old leather albums. "Did you know my father knew your mother? See, here the two of them are in a sled together. Remember the high winter snow? The bare-fingered trees pointing up the street from his house to hers? They might have married. But I'm glad they didn't. I wouldn't have cared to have you as a brother. It's better to have you a friend."

They talked of friendship and again as of old Vic found his words moving forward more freely with Loretta than ever with Cathy. "I'm married, Loretta. I've got the two boys. I want to work out an adjustment with Cathy if it can be done. But that needn't bar friendship between us. Nor between you and Cathy, if you know what I mean."

He had a moment's uneasiness wondering why she had turned her face from him. But the next instant she tossed back the hair that veiled her averted cheek and with moist lips and eyes lifted toward him, she murmured soft reassurance. She, too, felt that friendship mattered more than anything else.

"Damn friendship!" Cathy exploded in the therapy group. "Why should I take it? You go to Loretta's, Vic. And you slink home and confess and expect me to pat you on the back and say, 'Of course, little boy, go have a good time with your little girl friend' . . ."

"But Cathy, she's not my girl friend. She's your friend as much as mine."

"Like fun she is. She comes over, yes, with her platinum hair turning dark where it's parted and her smile as innocent as Lucretia Borgia's. She offers to help me sweep and sew and dust and she slyly leaves candy for the children. *Your* favorite kind. And I, like a fool, say, 'Hello, Loretta. How sweet of you. Thank you.' I'll play the game, Vic. I won't interfere with your friendship. But I want you, Vic, and I won't let her have you . . ."

"Why can't you see, Cathy? There's nothing more to it . . ." doggedly persistent. "If there were, I wouldn't have told you."

"Why *did* you tell her?" the doctor asked. There was not the slightest criticism in his tone. His words were like gentle fingers probing for what might lie beneath the surface.

"I wanted Cathy to know. I didn't want to do anything behind her back. I thought she would understand. That's what I want, her acceptance and her understanding, if you know what I mean."

"You make it sound as if you were going to mother to tell her about all the bad things you've done so she will assure you that everything's fine." The man who spoke seemed to be seeking an answer for himself. "I know how that is; it hits home. I've done it with my wife."

"Vic does sound as if he were taking Cathy as a mother," another put in. "He sounds the way I used to sound with my mother, *not* with my wife."

Vic looked from one to the other, over to the doctor, across to me, as if he were seeking to find in each the negation of some thought that was rising inside of him. He shook his head slowly. "But my mother never doubted me the way Cathy is doubting. She never challenged me. She never put me on the spot. My mother thought I was wonderful!" he protested. "My mother never made too many demands."

"Didn't she?" one of the women asked him. "You said at another session that you felt she demanded too much."

Vic hesitated a moment and then began talking, slowly considering what had been asked. "Yes, I guess in a way my mother did. In a way. I can't describe it exactly but it was a sort of demanding, I think. Like I've told you, I had to stoke the furnace, shovel the snow. I had to stay up late at night so she'd have company. But I liked that. My mother would do things with me; she'd tell me stories and show me picture books. We had a good friendsh . . . I mean, companionship . . ."

"Like you're trying now to reestablish with Loretta?"

But Vic did not seem to hear the question the doctor had put. His voice droned on until the doctor came in once more.

"What was it you said, Vic, about Cathy's demands?"

Vic looked puzzled. "Did I say anything? Let's see, what was it?"

He stopped and everyone waited. The pause lengthened into expectant silence.

"Yes," said Vic, "yes, I did say it." And then out of the abyss, like an earthquake's rumbling, "I'm just about fed up," he muttered. "I can't take it much longer. I can't stand Cathy's incessant demands. She needles and needles me. She's hypocritically sweet to placate me. But she's at me without end, forever wanting more than I can give. I'm beginning to feel I don't care whether I stay married or not. It's not worth it. This psychology business has gotten us all balled up. I used to think our marriage was perfect. . ." He stopped again and again looked puzzled. "Or did I?" He swallowed hard and looked straight at Cathy with his blue eyes deep in their sockets but not squinting. "No, I guess I didn't. There's always been something that's bothered me ever since the first night we were married . . ."

He stopped, leaving his sentence in mid-air.

"That's a funny thing to say," one of the group members

caught the inference. " 'Ever since the first *night,*' you said, not the first *day* you were married."

Vic looked down at the rug. "I guess at night she has seemed worse. At any rate she *is* worse at night now. She doesn't realize what it takes out of a person, trying to build up a business. She doesn't realize how tired I get and she just goes on demanding and demanding. She wants me to make love to her when I'm worn out. She keeps after me. Even when I'm asleep, she tries to get closer, and she knows how I hate that. I always have."

He shifted his body restlessly, uncrossed and re-crossed his legs. "Especially when she snores!"

He swallowed again and his voice dropped lower. "I like to be close when I'm awake. But once I've fallen asleep I can't stand it. Cathy knows how I am. If she gets close and I wake up and she happens to be snoring, I feel somehow that I'm going to be strangled or smothered. All I want to do is get up and run."

Into the circle of faces tenseness had crept. They waited in silence, feeling Vic's panic.

He cleared his throat. "So when I fall asleep I want to be sure I'm at a distance. I want to say, 'By God, Cathy, leave me alone!' But what's the use? She just keeps persisting." His voice was stronger, the edge of anger pushing through. "She keeps on and on with incessant demands and I'm getting fed up. I don't see any way out, and I'm damned if I care."

When the doctor and I talked later we found ourselves in agreement. Cathy and Vic were less comfortable than when they were first in psychotherapy but they were coming to be more openly at grips with their problems. We hoped they would be able to go on. For this was essential if their problems were ever to be solved. During too many years they had

174

covered the cracks in their marriage as one might cover the cracks in a house with creepers, blind to the presence of the cracks and lamenting only the aphids on the vine. To no avail. For unless one can see the chinks in a wall, one cannot mend them. Vines that cover the cracks do not make them whole. The house still disintegrates with the passage of time.

In the beginning Vic had known that something was wrong with their marriage. Therapy did not bring this as new knowledge to him. He had in fact told it to me in his first interview. "I don't know why it is," he had said, "but our marriage isn't as happy as it should be."

Up to the present, however, he had been unable to face what it was that was wrong. Only now was he beginning to approach it. What explanation he had essayed had been based on false premises, as on Cathy's being too quiet, less stimulating, less companionable than Loretta. Working from false premises could lead only to faulty solutions. Getting at the real premises would be uncomfortable and painful. And yet it was the only way toward any solution that was valid and sound.

Would Vic pull back in fear and cover up again as people often do when they are about to expose to themselves that they have been using pseudo-troubles to keep the realer emotional conflicts from showing? He might even wish at this point to drop therapy although it was far too unfinished to yield any lasting results. Unconsciously he might prefer to reinstate the pseudo-troubles in place of the truer yet more frightening ones he was approaching, turning his attention to the blight on the outside rather than to the graver trouble behind.

In their marriage Vic and Cathy had each helped the other to cover the inner troubles, though not to solve them. For one thing, because of the envy of her brother and because of other things which were still unclear, Cathy had not wanted Vic to be a man. This had dovetailed with Vic's fear of his own manhood. It had enabled him to cover the fear. But it did not solve the problem. Vic had been left seeking the self-esteem that comes to a man only as he feels himself a man in manhood's estate. Long before entering therapy, Vic had attempted two affairs to prove his virility, only to find that he could not. Even now he could not with Cathy. He would not with Loretta. Or was he using the would-not to cover the could-not?

Cathy was no longer content with the old pattern. She was demanding now, trying to push and prod Vic into giving her the gift of his manhood. But prodding does not beget love. Would she find out why she was choosing this way? Why she was beating down what she most wanted?

Would Vic work out of what there had been in his childhood that was still acting as a deterrent, keeping him in fear of being the man he deeply and essentially wanted to be?

We wondered about these things as we talked together, the doctor and I.

Meanwhile Vic went on seeing Loretta. And Cathy saw Blaine.

"You're wonderful, Cathy," over cocktails at a dim-lit table, hand reaching for hand, knees leaning toward each other one late afternoon. "You dance like a feather," with the sweetness of a waltz in their ears one evening when Vic had said he needed to work. "I like your house. It looks like you, Cathy. Neat and sleek!" another evening when Vic was out. "And your boys. They make me homesick for mine." . . . "How about dinner next week again, Cathy?" . . . "How about coming to my apartment tonight before I take you home?"

TWENTY-SIX

Kenneth knew his parents were having trouble. But he did not want to go on talking about it. Not for the present. He retreated to messing and smearing and made pictures which he declared he could not decipher. "Of course," he said, "they've got things in them but I'm not sure what."

He turned on me. "Don't you go poking into me, making me think bad thoughts."

"About what? About whom?"

"I can't tell you. *They'll* be angry."

"They'll be angry about what you want to do or say?"

He nodded. "Grams will be angry."

"Like she was in Peoria?"

"Like she was at Mother when Mother lost her pe—no, appendix. Like Mother is at Father now."

'Like you're afraid Mother might be at you?"

"I'm not mad at Mother. So, it's no use your thinking I am. I'll play a different game today. You say, 'It's Friday, the thirteenth.' "

"It's Friday, the thirteenth."

"That means it would be unlucky for me to do anything today. The kids took my marbles on Friday, the thirteenth. They ganged up with my brother against me at Gene's house. He's the boy up the street. His mother and father are having trouble. Maybe they'll get a divorce and either his mother or father will leave . . .

"And I hurt my finger, too, on Friday, the thirteenth. I hurt my arm on Friday, the thirteenth. So I'm not going to let you pull my thoughts out by their tails on Friday, the thirteenth."

"You're kind of afraid."

"Yes. You'll pull them out and chop their tails off."

I laughed and he laughed and he confided, "Only, thoughts don't have tails."

"No, Ken, but you have a sort of tail, don't you?"

"Uhuh." He nodded. "Only I know you won't cut it off like the doctor did my tonsils."

"No, I won't. Nobody will. And it's not really a tail."

His nod this time was more emphatic. "No, because it's welded on for keeps." He painted swiftly. "A thing-like-a-tail sticking into a thing-like-a-hole." All bright and yellow. "And," he paused, moving into a chuckle, "See, it's fastened here onto a thing like a boy!"

He drew a swift, strong line. "That's the boy's stomach. That's where it's welded on."

As if this had given him good courage, he came in the next time and immediately got to work. Intent on what he was doing, he fashioned a "club" out of clay. Bigger and bigger he

178

made it. He added chunk after chunk until most of the clay in the bucket had been used.

"There," he said, "it's simply enormous."

He stood up and with deep satisfaction apparent, he viewed his handiwork. "Yes, it's enormous. An enormous big club. And it's mine!"

"Tell me more about it."

"Well," he reflected, "it would seem like the trunk of an elephant."

He cocked his head to one side and then to the other, sizing the thing up. "Only it seems a little too long. Me and my ideas!"

Down on his hands and knees, he reshaped it. "There. I welded it over so it wouldn't be quite that long. If it stayed that long it might go through her. All the way through and out the other end. Out through her mouth. It might kill her."

"Perhaps that's what you and your ideas were doing when you made it too long."

His nod was emphatic. "Me and my ideas."

"You and those ideas do want to kill her sometimes."

He said nothing.

The silence in the room hung heavily over us. Still he said nothing. And then, in quick-moving decisiveness, he doubled his fists and made a thrusting motion, forward and up, as if he were running a spear through an enemy. There was no smile on his face now. His teeth were clenched as tight as his fists. His eyes were cruel slits, the brows scowling down over them. "All the way through her and out through her mouth."

He drew out the spear and thrust it again and again. Viciously, with the hard energy of the killer, the back of his head and neck in a hard, straight line.

"There," he said finally, and his hands loosened but did not slack. They were firm and full of energy. So was the whole boy.

His battle was done.

He was kneeling over the great club on the floor. "Now I can get it to be its right size. The right size, you know, to have a baby."

He was rebuilding after the storm. The vanquishing hero, his enemy gone.

"Let's make a mother," he said, "with a baby inside her."

"Not a mean mother?"

"No. She's dead."

"You just killed her."

"Uh huh. This one's nice. Lets make her have a baby!"

He worked steadily, accompanying himself with a whispered whistle that sounded like, "Me and My Gal."

Out of clay he fashioned the mother, full-bellied and pregnant. Out of cardboard he made the baby, curved in the expectancy of birth.

"Hm. Hm. It doesn't look much like a baby. It doesn't even look like a reasonable facsimile thereof. But it is. It's a baby all right."

He surveyed his creation. And once more, as earlier, placed the baby inside the mother.

"Now it's nine months later and out it comes.

"Make it come through the baby hole. The baby hole gets bigger. Ugghh, eee, uggg! What a tight squeeze. Eeee. Eeee. Here he is. Ga ga. He's a boy! He's mine and mother's. In my imagination. Not really real!"

He held the baby in the cup of his hand, smiling down at it. And then he looked up at me and laughed, full-throated and hearty. "Me and my thoughts!"

TWENTY-SEVEN

At last, after two years of therapy, Kenneth had shown the ultimate intent that had lain covered for so long: the wish to get rid of the mean mother and to possess the good mother. At last he could avow that this double wish applied to his own mother, not just to *a* mother; not to *any* mother but to *his*.

This is every child's wish, though the push and pull of it may be less violent. This was our wish, too, in the forgotten time behind the curtain of available memories.

Every mother is two mothers to a child. The mother who denies, the mother who grants less than a child yearns for— this mother he wants to eradicate. The mother who gives, who is loving, who understands and cherishes—this mother he

181

wants to own for himself. To her he wants to be "onliest." The onliest to suckle and nuzzle when he is tiny; the onliest to be held in sheltering arms. The onliest, later, if he is a son, to possess in the fantasy of marrying, just as the small daughter turns, if all goes well, to the father and murmurs wishfully, "We'll get married, Daddy, when I get big." Since the parent can never give himself to the child as fully as wishes demand, the child inevitably in his mind sees the parent as partly mean.

In his mind a child makes a mother more mean or less mean according to his fantasied wishes and needs as well as according to what he has actually known. The same with a father.

Again and again Kenneth had approached the conscious facing of his wish to get rid of his "mean" mother and the bigness of his demands. Again and again he had backed away. But through the repeated attempts, he had at last gained courage enough to look at his feelings for what they meant in their ultimate intent. The repetition of his *theme and variations* had been a necessary part of his therapy, as in most people's, in order to work through to the point where he could take the conscious impact of his wish's aim. Even though we had very gradually approached the ultimate baring of his unconscious desire to get rid of his mean mother, the fear of what killing her might portend in terms of actually losing his good mother along with the mean mother, had struck him after he was home. This became clear in his next session.

He came in with the very slightest whisper of a wheeze, barely perceptible but a wheeze no less. He slumped down onto the floor of the playroom without getting anything from the closet with which to play.

He didn't want to talk. He couldn't remember what he had

lone in the last session. "What was it?" he wondered, looking
puzzled. No, he couldn't recall any of it. And nothing had
happened at home to upset him either. He didn't want to do
anything, say anything, remember anything. No, he declared,
nothing was wrong. He reminded me of the little-boy-pulled-
into-himself who had come in two years before.

"If you ask me, I think you scared yourself last time into
the wheezes!" I ventured.

He regarded me stonily. Then anger flared. "Well, if you
have to pull my thoughts out, I've been mad at Brad. I wanted
to punch him in the nose. Only I couldn't, because I was
afraid of being scolded by YOU."

"Then you're really mad at me."

"Yes," emphatically, with all trace of the wheeze gone. "I'd
like to tell you off. Bawl you out. Why do you have to butt in
and disturb things?"

"You blame me for having disturbed your thoughts. Mad
because you would have liked to keep on thinking way down
inside you that you were having that baby with mother. And I
disturbed the idea!"

He nodded. "And so I feel like bawling you out. That's
all."

"Nothing more violent?"

"If I did, then you . . . No, *she* . . . she wouldn't take care
of me. She'd guess or find out somehow, and she'd send me
away."

At last this fear was out and in the open—this old fear so
terrible that it had played a big part in making Kenneth block
his hostility and keep it in. This fear had sprung up stark before Brad's birth when his mother had screamed that she did
not want another boy, when he had seen what he had sensed
much earlier, that she had not wanted him. His muscles had

caught this fear from her muscles' tensions when he had nuz
zled and found her breasts dry and when, despite the meticu
lous care that she gave him, he had apprehended her essentia
inability to give of herself and her love. This fear had spelled
loss and desertion. A fear that no child can bear.

His eyes now were wide and frightened.

"That idea makes you terribly scared!"

He did not move. He did not answer. But as I watched him
I saw the slow tears creep into his eyes. Down his cheeks they
trickled. They were the first tears I'd seen him shed.

There he sat on the bare brown floor of the play-room
alone with his sorrow. Not tight or cringingly backing away
Not wheezing. But meeting his thoughts and fears with a nat
ural, full sorrow. Strong enough not to seek refuge in me
Strong enough to bear his sorrow himself.

After a little while, he pulled a dirty handkerchief from
his pocket and wiped his face, streaking it with grime. A
smile came slowly, and in a low voice he began to muse. "
can't club her. I can't poke her. But I *can* do other things. And
I just will. When I'm mad I'll do different things to annoy
her. I won't eat what she wants me to. I'll turn on the washing
machine while she's not looking and I'll plug the lights in her
bedroom so they won't light when she wants them. And then
later when she's trying to go to sleep, I'll turn the lights on
And I'll go cut the clothes line. And I'll wheeze."

"And that will irritate her?"

"You guessed it."

"And it will hurt you also!"

"Yes, you've said it. I guess it's a no-good idea. But . . ."

"But," I picked up the wishful note in his voice, "it's a
idea you still sort of like."

He looked relieved and easy as he rose from the floor and

went to the play closet. He brought out the mother he had made the time before and the baby.

"Here's the baby who was born last week," he said. "I'll make him grow bigger." He got out clay and fashioned a boy. "He's a day old and a week old and a month old and a year." He kept making him bigger. "And now he's about four or five, I don't know exactly, maybe just three. But he wants to go into his mother. Only he can't. That's the daddy's job."

He took more clay and fashioned a father. "Now the daddy and the mother, they'll have a baby in the proper way."

Thus Kenneth gave his mother back to his father. Thus he stepped off his magic carpet and set foot on the ground.

TWENTY-EIGHT

Cathy struggled with herself as time passed: I want a man. I want a man. A man who gives me something; who doesn't leave me empty. Blaine was constantly in her thoughts. Blaine with his hard, demanding eagerness. How long would she want to push him away? Or did she want to? Should she? Shouldn't she?

Cathy struggled with Vic: Give me more, Vic. Why don't you give me more?

"I put over a big deal today, Cathy." Blaine's voice on the telephone held the lift of accomplishment in it. "How about celebrating with me tonight?"

Cathy succeeded in getting a neighbor to stay with the

children since Vic was working. She dressed in the dark blue spring taffeta and almost upset the perfume bottle with the trembling of her hands. She needed no rouge; she noticed in the mirror the high flush on her cheeks.

After dinner they wound into the hills on their way home through the pass. Cathy felt the long frame of Blaine's body hard against her side as he pulled her toward him. She drew in a deep breath and let her mind slide where it would. To the flowers he'd brought her, fragrant in their whiteness on her shoulder. The restaurant he'd chosen with the coziness of their table hidden in the niche behind the brick hearth. The captain's obsequious manner. "Cocktails, surely. Double martinis!" . . . "Wine with the dinner, of course, Mr. Ross." . . . Blaine's commanding, sure way of ordering. And the sureness of his hand on her elbow as he'd helped her back into the car. It was then she'd had a swift premonition that tonight her life was going to change.

Blaine pulled to a stop where the hills jutted out above the city of flickering lights. Neither of them spoke. The hum of traffic far below was an accompaniment to the crickets singing. To the pain and pleasure of wanting. To the sliding away of the trees into blackness as Blaine's mouth closed over hers.

As if in a dream she felt his hands unbuttoning her dress. She was a little girl, her mother away in the hospital, her father taking care of her. She'd fallen asleep in his arms, gazing at the stars outside the window, and now he was carrying her off to bed, undressing her in her limp, small helplessness.

She shivered when the horn of a passing car jarred into her and pulled Blaine's head into an upright, stark silhouette.

"We're not children, Cathy," she heard his voice with a hard metallic note in it. "Like silly kids on a mountain top, having to park to get in their loving."

He buttoned up her dress and started the car on its winding way. "We're going to my apartment."

He held her nearer, her head on his shoulder, her eyes closed against her thoughts.

These things Cathy told me and painted in swift words the evening's subsequent events.

The strange dancing beat of her heart. The throb of the motor and the veins in her throat. Was she alive? Was she dead? Never more yielding than in the not-there feeling of now. But there was a bright silver string strung through her, pulling her entrails into taut knotting. And there was a silver ball behind her eyes, pressing up into the top of her head. . . . I want to. Can I? . . . Don't think. Let things happen. . . . Cathy, stop trembling. Cathy, let go.

She did not feel the ground under her feet when they got out. She was standing on clouds that had no substance. They lifted and swayed.

And then, she was leaning over the curb, retching. Ignominiously ill.

"I'm sorry, Blaine. The wine and the cocktails."

"Come on up, Cathy. You'll feel better in a few minutes. The curves in the road, that's what did it. But I'll make you some coffee and you'll soon be all right."

She put out a hand and touched his arm, feeling the firmness through his sleeve. "Please not tonight, Blaine. I—I don't know what happened. I feel so darn sick."

When he let her out at her door, his face, she thought, looked hard and ugly. His hands, she thought, were tight like fists about to hit her. And suddenly, from under the misery in her, a fiery streak ran up her back.

His last words had been that he would call her. But the next day had passed and the next, and no call had come.

TWENTY-NINE

"I can't club her!" Kenneth had said. "But I can do other things."

"If I were Hamburger," he elaborated one day, "I'd show her I was angry. I'd jump on her bed and get paw marks all over it. I'd get real mad and growl and bark. I'd chew up her purse and get mud on it. I'd be a real mad and happy Hamburger. Real happy to be mad."

He looked at me soberly. "I'd like to be like that. I'd like to do things, too, to show her how I feel. I'd like to be a real-happy-to-be-mad-Kenneth. But if I got too outspoken it would just get me into a mess of trouble. I can't do it with her. I know that. But I can get the mad out in here with you."

He became freer and easier in reporting what had gone on at home and in the neighborhood. "My boy friend Gene took

189

me to a movie. He treated me. I feel more like a friend!" . . .
"And me and a couple of other boys got some flower seeds and
planted them in the empty lot." . . ."And we're working on a
model airplane."

He was freer, too, in expressing his feelings. He was angry
at his mother when she was late to meet him at the dentist's
one afternoon. He was angry when she forgot to pick him up
at school as she'd promised to do. He was angry at her and
at his father when they proposed taking back his room for
their study and moving him in again with Brad.

"It makes me furious," he announced, glowering. "It'll put
me right down again at Brad's level, three years younger than
I am. "I'll have to turn the lights off earlier and turn the radio
off earlier. Just the idea of the whole business makes me mad
. . . They don't care how much Brad disturbs me. I don't know
what I'll do if I have to move in with that brat . . ."

He stopped and a crafty look came into his face. "Oh, yes,
I do know. I'll cough and I'll sneeze and I'll wheeze. I'll get
the asthma again. I'll annoy them with it every night. Every
night about every half-hour I'll call them in and I'll be such
a nuisance keeping Brad awake that he'll be all peevish and
shrieky and they won't be able to stand either of us together,
and then they'll *have* to give me back my own room . . ."

Even though he thought he could not manage to talk about
it to his parents, he had.

At dinner that evening when Brad was especially silly, Ken
saw an opening. He threw a glance in Brad's direction, and
then turning to his mother, he announced with utter disdain,
"That there's my brother. I love him. I could murder him.
And if you put me into that room with him, I will."

He reported to me a few days later, "I was surprised. She
took it O.K."

He grew more expansive. "It's really remarkable. She really can take it from me better than she used to. I guess because she's learning to bring her own crossness out in little fire-cracker explosions. She doesn't hold it all in the way she did. You should see her at home sometimes. She looks like a witch.

"But it's still hard for me to say things to her. It's still easier to say them to you."

He looked pensive. And then very slowly, as if he were pushing to see his direction through fog, he struggled to bring into words what had long been one of his greatest fears. "Sometimes I want to let go. Over some little nothing, almost. Some little thing happens; only it isn't little when it gets to me. It seems big. I guess because it sets off something *big* inside me. The biggest wish to SOCK that you ever knew. It's so big that if I socked anybody with that much steam I—I— think I'd explode."

In great simplicity, Kenneth had elucidated what many people never come to understand. He had been so afraid that he might act on his inner anger and carry out to the full what it dictated that he had kept himself tightly in check. Immobilized almost. So afraid had he been of the push and the force of hostility in him that he had closed up and denied that any was there. In his unconscious mind, however, it had continued to propel him until again and again he had turned it back onto himself, punishing himself for the bad wishes and thoughts, getting sick, feeling guilty, cringing and failing.

If a child's emotional hungers are satisfied by his mother in the helpless beginnings of life when he cannot fend for himself, then he can take in better stride the necessary denials which must be imposed on him as he grows. If he were to put the matter into words, he might say, "I get angry, yes, at big people for their forbidding me things I want. But still I know they are fundamentally with me and for me. They care about me. They proved that to me when I was small."

On the other hand, when forbiddings follow early deprivations and a child has not come to the place where he feels he can trust his parents to love and understand him, he is apt to feel they deny him because they don't care about him. Then hurt and anger and rage and fury mount far more stormily. They must be barricaded all the more tightly. It's as if he said to himself, "I must not even look to see that these feelings exist. If I acknowledge them, they may burst and destroy me and my world."

Kenneth, however, had looked. With me to support him, he had come through pain and fear to a place of seeing. The pain and fear had grown small enough to endure, and Kenneth had built inner courage enough to tolerate the remnants that still were there and always would be. The trust in me that he had come to feel so profoundly had helped him to make up for his earlier lack of trust in his mother and father. It had helped him move forward toward trust in himself.

Now, since he trusted himself more securely, he could trust himself to manage feelings that he had not felt capable of managing earlier.

Before coming into therapy, he had built up a way of managing himself that was in truth self-demolishment. His way of checking himself had not lain in control but in paralysis. He had virtually immobilized effective functioning in his fear lest unwanted feelings come through. As a result he had not been able to bring out normal aggressiveness. The drive and the push had been so checked that he could not even tackle school subjects with the verve that comes when feelings flow freely into any act. It was as if he had posted a demon of punishment at the streets' intersection, always keeping the "Go" sign off and the "Stop" sign on.

But now he felt it less necessary to call on the demon. Kenneth felt himself more able to judge and choose and guide what he should do. He could use his eyes and look over the terrain and take into account what the traffic could bear. He could say to himself, "I'll not go up that street; it's better not to. I'll move along this other street instead. The first street's not safe; the second one is." He could say to himself, "It's not possible to let my feelings run along this action pathway. But along this other one, it's all right.

"I can't let my feelings run out in the act of clubbing my mother. That way is no good.

"But I can talk to my mother sometimes about my feelings. Though only very occasionally.

"I can talk my feelings out to you and to myself...

"I've been mad at my mother lots. I was mad at her the other day because she promised me I could go to the store with her and then she went off and completely forgot that I was waiting. I'd like to have called her an idiot. But I knew if I did, she'd get too sore. So I drew little idiot pictures and knew in my mind who they were."

Or again, "I'd like to sock her really. But she's a woman and so I can't. I went and socked my ball, though, all around the block."

He could manage these feelings now more consciously without shoving them all into his unconscious mind. He had acquired the basis for true *self-control*—for managing the outflow of feelings, neither denying nor letting them run wild. He saw what he could do and what he could not do in more realistic terms.

Kenneth had seen too that he could not gain good, warm sensations in his body through possessing his mother. But the deep and human universal wish to experience body-feelings of pleasure was in him. He needed to know, just as all of us need to know, that these can exist without a person's having to feel dirty and bad. He needed to know, just as all of us need to know, that he would have to steer and control the outlets in accordance with our culture's demands, again not by blocking or denying or paralyzing them, but by finding legitimate action-pathways for them to travel along.

We talked about this just as we talked about finding outlets for his feelings of anger. I reiterated what he already knew: that he wouldn't be able to make love to a woman until he was big. But that of course he would think of it and wish that he were already big all the time of his growing.

He made a finger painting in gorgeous colors, warm and glowing magenta-red against a background of acquamarine. A great shaft ran up the center with hands curved around it.

He stood off and surveyed it, and nodded in quiet satisfaction. "A penis with hands touching it. It feels good."

Then, dreaming forward into the future and back into the past, he bridged the time span between with the first marriage dream of every small boy. He worded it now without confusion, knowing it could not be. "Sometimes it wants to go into the mother's baby hole. But naturally it can't."

And then, musingly, he recalled other ways toward solution that he had essayed. "Remember, when I used to poke into the big job hole? I would pretend then that I was poking in the mother's baby hole, exploring, sort of. Trying to find out what was in there.

"And then when I thought how bad it was to want to go

194

into the baby hole the hands would grab and hurt the penis to hold it back and punish it. That's the red . . ."

I wondered if I saw him flinch, ever so slightly? Were there still in the red of blood's tinge, some things that frightened?

He could see now, however, that hurting himself was not the answer. "That's no use!" he declared. "It's better to make it feel good with the touching. In bed at night. Instead of counting sheep!"

Here again was a legitimate action-pathway, owning up to the feelings and controlling their outflow; not needing to let sex any more than aggression remain a dark demon, unmanageable and bad.

"I can't poke her. But I can do other things."

He had brought out the wish and we'd worked together. The baby wish of dependency on one hand, to push all of himself into his mother, to crawl back into her sheltering body. The man-dream of aggressive independence on the other hand. The wish to conquer and possess. He had faced his fear of letting either side of the impulse flow out into action. The fear of being engulfed and eaten as the baby guppies had been eaten by their mother. The fear of injury to a part of his body, his leg being amputated, hurt by an enemy whose identity even now he had not grasped.

He had explored his feelings and the fantasies enough to glimpse the comforting fact that he could keep them imagined. He had met the stirring in him enough to know that *he could impose restrictions on himself without imposing punishment.*

Kenneth had seen that he could not bring out his wish to "poke" into his mother. Not directly. But there were some

195

more "reasonable" ways of solving the wish, some action-pathways along which it might legitimately go.

"Noises are more reasonable than noses going into ears," he announced one day.

"How do you mean, Ken?"

"Well, when Hamburger barks, his noises go into your ears. That's more reasonable than his little wet nose poking in."

I nodded and waited.

"My noises go into my mother's ears," he elaborated, "just like Hamburger's bark. I used to poke coughing and wheezing noises into her ears. Now I poke different kinds of noises in. The kind she likes better. Good noises, like when I told her yesterday that I'd gotten a spelling prize in school and good grades."

I commented that he was poking his nose into books apparently. He laughed and said he was getting quite nosy. At school, too, he'd wanted to find out what a couple of boys were whispering about and he'd gotten into a fist fight. "Not a bad one. Just enough to show them I could get in on the show. Then, you know? The one I fought with deserted the other and whispered to *me*!"

I checked with the principal. "Yes. He actually did fight. I'd seen it coming; he's been ever so much more aggressive. Fortunately, I'd prompted his teacher that if he should fight, she should just stand by and not let it get too hot. But if possible not to stop him. He's needed so badly to get to where he *could* fight. He held his own, too, the other day when a boy tried to take his place in the line. He said 'No' and actually pushed the other youngster away. And he's getting along better now on the playground; takes more part in games and has made some good friends."

"How about taking a test?" I asked him one day.

"One of those I.Q. things?"

"Yes."

"To see how my mind works?"

"To see how well it's been poking its nose into all kinds of business, finding out about this and that."

He took it in stride as a challenge, eager to see what the test was about.

I was not surprised when the results came to me.

This boy, who two years earlier had been labeled too low to pass with the rest of the children, this boy who had been told to repeat his grade because his score was "only one hundred and eight"—*this boy's intelligence quotient now showed above one hundred and forty.*

I felt as if a gift had been laid in my lap.

Kenneth was now able to use the intelligence that had always been his. It was no longer blocked and tied down along with feelings that had to be held in. It wasn't the test result of itself that pleased me, but rather what it indicated of the general freeing in Kenneth. The test result was a sign that things were going well. So was the absence of asthma. Kenneth had had no attack for over two months, ever since the session after he had painted the great elephant club that had killed his "bad" mother.

Kenneth put into his own words a few weeks later what was happening. "I think I'm getting healthy," he announced. "If this keeps up, I'll soon be able to get a Life Insurance policy."

But Cathy and Vic were having a hard time and in my mind lay the question: was Kenneth healthy enough to take in his stride the things that might come?

197

Blaine finally called Cathy. But not until resentment over his not calling had grown big inside her.

"How are you, Cathy? I've been a brute not to have phoned you sooner. But I've been so darn busy. That big deal, you know."

"Of course, Blaine!" Cathy's voice was as smoothly cold as silk. "Next to that big deal, why should you have wasted time thinking about little me?"

"But I *have* been thinking about you, Cathy. It isn't that." Uncharacteristically he seemed to hesitate. Then, quickly retrieving, he asked, "How about dinner tomorrow night?"

"I'm sorry, Blaine. I can't."

Cathy heard herself as if she were listening to another

person. The anger in her was so pressing that she automatically used the glassy surface to keep it covered.

Blaine got the coolness. "I don't blame you for being sore, Cathy." His voice took on the muffled note of trying to prevent others from hearing. "Forgive me, dear?"

She sat frozen and did not answer.

"Come on, Cathy. Don't act that way." And after a few moments more of tormented silence, "If you don't feel like talking to me now, call me when you do. Any time, either here or at my place."

Again he waited. She still did not answer. She sat tight and stiff, fighting back the angry tears.

"Just remember, Cathy, I'm not the type to give up easily. If I don't hear from you, you'll hear from me."

She heard the phone click.

"Hello! Blaine!...Blaine!" Her voice rose. She looked at the receiver, disbelieving its silence. She clicked the telephone. "Hello, Blaine, where are you?" But there was only the disconnected wire's empty buzz.

I wondered how much Ken sensed of what was happening until he came in one day with a worried look. He was frankly anxious but he was not wheezing.

"I'd rather not go in the playroom today," he said. "Could we go into your office?"

I nodded and as we went in together I felt that he was reaching from ten-year-old seriousness into something far beyond.

"I need to talk to you," he said, "about my mother. She's been upset. I don't know why exactly. I don't know what it is. But she's been taking it out on all different things. She's been cross at everybody.

"I have a good idea it's really at Father. She's been trying to get things off her chest at him. But he kind of stymies her because he's so pulled back. He keeps his feelings too small on the outside. And then they get too big on the inside. And that's no good.

"I wish he'd learn to fight more in the open. Then he and my mother would get it out between them and it wouldn't seem so bad. Then she wouldn't have to splash it out on us the way she does."

And after a few pensive moments, "If you ask me, Dorothy, I think my father is running away."

And so Vic was. He was working early and late. And in between at all hours he was seeing Loretta. "It's good to drop in, Loretta," sinking back in the easy chair. "Thanks for the highball." . . . "I don't know what I'd do without your friendship. It's good to find peace."

In the group, Vic had several times now come out with resentment toward Cathy. But it was hard for him to sustain it and to stand up for himself in the face of her pushing demands.

"I feel as if I'm a dead duck when she starts in with her needling. No matter what I do it's never enough. I'd just as soon quit. As soon as I get the paint-job done on the house I'll have to check out."

"Why not now, Vic?"

"Because I wouldn't want to leave the house half-finished, if you know what I mean."

"Then why," growled one of the men in the group, "why leave *yourself* half-done?"

Ken, too, felt the half-done, uncertain quality of his father.

"My father really should stand up and be more angry when my mother criticizes him. He shouldn't be such an in-between man."

Cathy fought with herself: Should she call Blaine? Shouldn't she? She wanted to. She didn't want to. If she called him, she recognized how he would take it, and that it would in fact be a kind of promise.

"Why did things have to happen the way they did?" she moaned. "Why did I have to get sick just at the crucial moment?"

"How about it, Cathy?" I asked.

As she pressed through the thoughts that followed, one thing crept out of the fog: she had wanted a man and she had turned him down. The illness which had overcome her that evening had not been simply her body's reaction to curves and wine. The retching had been her body's way of saying: "I'm afraid."

Blaine didn't call. And Vic ran from her. And Cathy's vindictiveness grew.

Ken saw it.

"She criticizes my father much too much. She raises things from the dead. She said, for example, that the night when I was being born, father sat outside and figured on his engineering stuff. She made real sarcastic remarks about it to him the other night. And he just sat.

"Finally I stuck my nose in. I said, 'That issue should have been settled years ago.'

"What did she want him to do, anyway? Pace around and worry?"

One day it dawned on me. A new thing was happening. As Cathy's regard for Vic decreased, her praise of Ken began increasing.

She brought it to me. She brought it to the group.

"Ken's done so well in school. You should hear what the principal says about him." . . . "He's so noticing. So keen. And so much more open. He doesn't seem like a child, the way he thinks and reasons! He's wonderful the way he understands."

Again and again, "Ken is wonderful!" Until ultimately Cathy reached in and brought out the essence of what she was feeling. She put it quite simply and tersely, "I can talk to Ken like to a man."

She wanted her man. And since she felt that Vic and Blaine both had failed her, Cathy was now turning to Ken.

THIRTY-ONE

Not long after, Kenneth came in very depressed. He was wheezing slightly. Except for one other very light spell, this was the only evidence of asthma he had had in the six months that had passed since the session following the killing of his mean mother with his great elephant club. The other had come when we had cut down his therapy to once a week. He had taken the decrease in his sessions to mean that I was deserting him in a way similar to his mother's emotional desertion of him earlier, when out of her own hunger she had left him hungry. With a resurgence of the old fear that he might be shoved out altogether, he had blocked the hostility that had welled up toward me.

A dream, however, had told us it was there. In the dream he

saw a wicked witch who tried to push him over a cliff to get rid of him. She looked like his mother and me, he said, in weird combination. "I guess I felt you were pushing me out like she used to. And I was mad at you for it. Real mad," he avowed.

Then he'd gone into a fantasy he'd been harboring of being my child, of my taking him home to live with me. He, was angry at me because, by cutting down on his treatments, I was making it clear that his dream could not come true. I was the bad witch mother. "So that's what it was," he smiled. "Me and my wants!"

"And sometimes," I nodded, "those wants of yours get as big as an elephant's."

"Too big to be fed," he agreed. "And that's why I turned you into the ugly witch. It was *me* who wanted to push *you* over the cliff . . . or . . . *poke* you over, and not politely, either."

We had laughed at this, and I had noted again that as his anger vented itself, his breathing eased.

We knew clearly by now when he wheezed that it always meant he was failing to avow or admit some anger that he felt. I wondered as I looked at him today what there was on his mind.

"Unfortunately, I've got the wheezles," he said. "Only I can't quite put my finger on why!"

"Let's go after it," I suggested.

"O.K."

He wanted these days to lie down on the couch like his mother had told him some of the grownups did. I'd explained to him that when they lay down they let one thought bring on another, as on a linked chain where one link connected up with and hitched into the next. That he should let each thought that popped into his head come right out through his mouth. He had caught the idea readily.

The first thing he thought of today was Gene, his friend. Gene's father and mother had fought so much that the father had moved out. Now Gene's mother was getting a divorce.

"It's awfully hard on Gene. He has to get up terribly early and take a paper route. And his mother's dependent on him for the money he earns. The paper route I think would be fun. But not the burden. The responsibility is too big for a boy."

Then he decided he would have a movie show. He'd project the scenes out of his mind onto the blank wall in front of him and give me the happenings, scene by scene.

"The first scene," he began, letting his mind run its own course, "it's of a fight between my mother and Brad. Mother doesn't like Brad's disposition and she gets sore at him like she really did last night. It makes me feel I was in the middle, as if she expected me to do something about it. I was afraid of what might happen. That they would never forgive each other. That's the way it is in this movie. They never make up. And in the end, Brad runs away from home."

"There!" he announced. "Brad's eliminated."

"How does that make you feel?" I asked.

"I feel sorry," he grinned. Then added, "But if the truth were told, I feel glad. I've been sore at Brad. He's disturbing the whole family. He's disturbed the peace."

He went on ruefully, "Unfortunately, however, Brad's going away didn't help much. The next scene shows why. It's titled, 'Life Without Brad.'

"Mother goes around looking cross. She has an *after-grouch*. Whatever it was is still affecting the family and we're all unhappy. And finally there's a big war between Mother and Dad. Mother finally lets the soreness inside run away with her. And Daddy doesn't try to stop her. It makes me feel I'm in the middle, as if she expects me to do something about it. And I get even more afraid than when she has bad feelings toward Brad."

Then very wistfully, "I wish I knew more what was really wrong between them. I think they're still hiding things to themselves. Fights they haven't worked out into the open. I wish they would. It's so much easier, the part you can see . . . Because then you know how big the storm is, instead of worrying how big it will be when it comes . . .

"Well, finally in this movie they find they can't get enough ironed out and they have to get a divorce like Gene's folks did."

He hesitated and visibly tightened. Then, with obvious struggle, he went on. "Now the next scene . . ."

Again came the hesitations. As I waited my mind ran forward. He had eliminated Brad. In the next scene no doubt he would eliminate his father. He and his mother would then be alone together. The ultimate would be accomplished.

To my surprise he announced, "The next scene is titled, 'Life Without Mother.' I went with Dad when they split up. That was my only solution, you see. I had to . . ."

"Why, Ken?"

"Because if I went with her it would be too hard."

He looked near to tears. "I want to give her credit. She tried! But she did just the wrong things. I don't know just how. I see a big tank on the wall now, rolling toward me. It's going to roll over me, over my chest. It's going to smother me so I can't breathe . . ."

"Like you're afraid Mother might if you were alone with her?"

"Yes!" In his voice was the joy of sudden relief.

Then the anger came pouring, and again as it came out the wheezing cleared. "I'm mad at Mother. I'm sore at her and at Father, too. He should act bigger than Brad and not have to duck out. He's bundled his feelings up much too long. He should talk and tell his side and get things off his mind and say what he feels like saying. Instead he falls back without half getting started. You'd think with his being so big he wouldn't have to be such a little man.

"He makes me worry about when I grow up. I don't want to be like that. I want to express myself and be stronger. Sometimes I think if I could see him be bigger, I'd know better how to be bigger myself."

He was much concerned in the sessions that followed with wanting a sturdier father, big in emotional strength and manliness as well as in size. He felt a need for this big, sturdy father, not only to give him the image of what a man should be to shape himself after but also to protect him, as it were, from the intensity of his mother's new turning to him.

"You know," he confided one day, "it's hard. Mother puts me in the position of responsibility of Daddy. But I don't have the authority of Daddy."

"One reason she does it though, I think, is because Daddy doesn't seem like a man. He clams up too much. And it makes a mess in our home."

He took a deep breath and let his thoughts run on. "Brad capitalizes on it. He goes all haywire. He feels he can get away with anything. I think if Brad saw Daddy coming to his senses and out of his in-between-ness, he would come to his senses too. And that would make it easier for him. *If Daddy were stronger, he'd be helped by Daddy not to do what he wants to do in himself.*"

I asked if Ken were not also talking about himself.

He looked thoughtful. "Yes, I am. If Daddy were stronger with Mother, he'd help me too."

He went on to relate that he had read in the newspapers about a sex crime. A father had seduced his daughter. This reminded him of a dream he'd had of a girl who looked like his mother. She had come along and asked him to marry her.

"If there could be a father-daughter deal like that," he said, "it would also be possible for there to be a mother-son deal. So it's not really impossible. But," he took a deep breath and grinned broadly, *"it's important to keep the possible impossible. I'm sure that I can."*

THIRTY-TWO

Kenneth could keep the possible impossible, although he went on feeling that it might be easier if he could count on his father for a limiting power that was not there now.

"If he were stronger, I could relax more. Things would be easier for me. I think he's got it in him all right."

And another time: "I wonder how he got so gummed up. I guess his parents didn't give him a chance. I wish he'd come out of himself, though, instead of pulling himself all in.

"Not that I think my mother's blameless. I don't. She needles him too much. But I think she'd let up if he'd show his feelings more openly. They're what she's after. Not only his gripes but his love.

"He's courteous, yes. But that's not all there is to loving. When I grow up, I'll show my wife I love her a lot, not just on and off but all the time. I'll be more sparkly than Daddy."

In spite of the problems that his father and mother had not yet worked out, Kenneth was doing all right.

"I seem to be able to take things better," he announced one day. "I haven't had real asthma for about a year."

Actually he had had no asthma for the past eight months except for the two very slight episodes I have recounted—the one when his therapy time had been reduced and the other when he'd felt his mother's turning to him as too heavy and threatening a burden. Both times he had briefly blocked the hostility. Against me because he didn't want to take a chance on losing me as he felt he had his mother. Against his parents because with the realization of his father's weakness the danger came too close of carrying out his own wish to kill and overcome him and shove him out. He expressed this aptly himself. "If he stays half a man, then if I wanted to some day, I could shove him out. Or, if I couldn't alone, I could get mother to. She's so much on my side. Together we could as a combination, she and me. But I'd rather not."

I wondered if, in the back of his mind there might not lie the fear that even though weak, his father would then be goaded beyond endurance, and might do him harm.

As for his resentment, it was now an open book from which he could easily draw excerpts; the push of it did not seem too big any longer for him to handle and steer.

"Things go on and on between them. I wish they could get more therapy, my Daddy especially. The other day when he and I were building a model plane, working together, just the two of us, I told him he had too many worries and that he ought to tell them more to you. Perhaps if I gave up my times with you, he could spend that money on times for himself. I told him I thought he needed it. I can just see him sitting in the group with his shoulders hunched over, clammed up like he clams up at home. If he could come in more times, perhaps you could help him loosen up like you've helped me . . ."

I wondered if his generosity might not be prompted by his own feelings of being stronger. So I said that perhaps there were other reasons why he, Ken, preferred not to come any more. Reasons of his own, aside from his father. Perhaps he felt he really didn't need me any more.

He nodded thoughtfully. "I think I feel I don't need you regularly. I see things clearer. I used to think, for instance, that Brad was such a big nuisance I needed you to help me stand up against him, I guess because I wanted him evacuated and didn't dare let myself go. Now my expectations are different and I can handle him for myself. I don't want him evacuated—at least not all the time—because I have so much fun fighting with him and arguing and feeling superior. Though at times," ruefully, "Brad is superior."

"And you can't be the onliest as you've wanted to be."

He nodded. "But somehow it doesn't matter as much."

We went on to plan and he said, "I would like to be able to call you, though, when things get too hot. Do you think we could manage that kind of arrangement? Then if I felt the asthma starting, if it ever does again, I could get over here before it got bad. Or if other things were bothering in a pressing kind of way that I couldn't manage myself, I could come before they piled up.

"It would be a good feeling to know I could come whenever I needed you. But I'm real busy at school now and real busy playing. When I started with you I didn't need time for playing. I didn't have one true friend then. Now I have lots.

211

I think now I need more time for myself and my friends."

We decided that we'd have a kind of try-out for three weeks to see how it felt without me, and that then he would come in to report.

He arrived in good spirits. "Yes," he said, "I think I can manage even though my father and mother do go on and on. At least I don't have to hide from myself any more that they do get me mad the way they are."

I asked, "How do you mean, Ken?"

"Well," he answered with thoughtful deliberation, "it's this way: Mother keeps making everything bigger. Father keeps making everything smaller. But, as for me, things are more according to size. I guess I'm further along than they are because we started with me when I was younger. For me the big troubles *are* big. But they're there and I have to stand them. The little troubles, fortunately, aren't too big any more."

He paused for a moment and then resumed very seriously, "I seem more in proportion. Yes, that's a good word for it. More in proportion. That's what I am."

THIRTY-THREE

The months passed and winter rolled around again. Vic had not seen Loretta for over a week. Late one evening he phoned her, he was tired and blue. "I need you to cheer me up."

When he arrived at Loretta's, he let himself in the un-latched door. A log was burning in the fireplace. A plate of small sandwiches lay on the coffee table. From the bedroom Loretta called out, "That you, Vic? I'll be there in a moment." He took off his overcoat and latched the door.

She came in, her hair, almost gold-white, falling straight to her shoulders, her robe, almost white with a satiny gold sheen, clinging to her body, her long nails gilded with a new polish she had just put on. Long, gold pendants hung from her ears.

213

She crossed the room and stretched out both hands to him. "You look dead, Vic, and shivery. How about coffee with brandy to warm you up?"

Vic felt suddenly eased. The tightness dropped from his shoulders and his tongue slid into speech. "You look gorgeous, Loretta. You're a sight for sore eyes. I didn't know how much I'd been missing you."

Without volition his arms went around her and he felt her body, lithe and slim and yielding against him. "Oh, Lorie, Lorie." He groaned as he kissed her hair.

She slipped away from him and beckoned him to the low chair, poured the coffee and brandy and settled herself on the floor at his feet. She wanted to know how his work was going. Were the problems on the Townsend job working out? "It seems such ages. There's so much to catch up on! Let's not ever be away from each other so long again!"

He smiled as if humoring a child, and pulled her head back against his knees.

He ran his hand through her hair, through the silk length of it as he had done many times. As his hand slipped over the smooth ends, he started. It was as if sudden surprise went through him that her hair did not reach further down. "I expected it suddenly to reach below her waist," he told me. "It came as a kind of shock that it stopped too soon."

The picture he had painted earlier of his mother's long hair reaching waist downward flashed into my mind then, and how he had relished the feel of it slipping through his fingers as he'd brushed it when he was a boy.

"Oh, Vic!" Loretta's voice held a plea and a sob mingling. Rising on her knees she turned toward him and flung her arms around his neck. "How much longer can we go on like this,

214

Vic? All this business of friendship and leaving love and sex out of it. It isn't natural. There have been nights and nights I've lain awake wanting and dreaming. Aching with the dream and the want."

She grasped his shoulders and shook him. "Vic, you've got to snap out of it. You don't owe Cathy anything more. She's a bitch the way she treats you. I've watched her. Peevish and demanding and cross. She's got the boys. I've got no one. I need you, Vic, Terribly. Please, Vic! Wake up."

He felt, he told me, as if he were a rag doll being shaken. Numb, without feeling. His tongue as large and bloated in his mouth as a man's strung from the gallows. This was happening to him but he was not in it.

As if through a screen of transparent net making the scene hazy, he saw Loretta's face twisting. He saw her burst into tears and heard her deep pulling sobs. She was wild in her crying. Bereft and abandoned. Pleading for life.

And then, as if he were plodding out of an abyss, fumbling for firm ground, he heard himself saying, "There, there, Lorie, darling. Come over here." With his arm about her, he led her to the wide divan and folded her in his arms.

She pulled off her earrings, dropped them jarringly on the coffee table, put her head in his shoulder and sobbed and sobbed.

"Please, Vic, take me. Please, please, Vic!"

He went on stroking her hair, murmuring to her not to cry.

To himself he thought, and the thought ran through him: Why not? Why not for good and always? Why go on this way, clinging to some foolish idealistic hold-over from childhood? Why stay with Cathy when he could be with Loretta? The struggle between Cathy and himself, the hard battling out of silence and the silent battling before—all of it had made such a shambles of their marriage. The vows in the little church in the country town where they'd been married were the lost whisper of a promise. Why try to keep the form when the essence was gone?

"Leave her, Vic! Won't you? Please, darling, come to me."

"Maybe, Lorie," he heard himself murmuring to assuage her and to reassure himself. "Maybe, darling. Now keep quiet and try to relax."

He felt the tautness in her go limp as he lay down and pulled her gently to him. "There! There! Darling!" He wanted only to quiet her. The rest could wait.

How long they lay there he never knew, until finally and imperceptibly he heard her breathing grow regular and felt the small twitching message of sleep passing into her. Her arms fell from around him and she turned on her back.

He raised himself on his elbow and looked down on her. Her lips were pouting slightly. Her breathing came a little heavily from the clogging of her nose after tears, and a small whistling sound passed through them like a whispered snore.

His throat constricted. His chest tightened. His mouth went dry. Sheer panic filled him. One impulse alone gripped him. Nothing else mattered: he had to get away.

He rose carefully so as not to wake her, crossed the room and looked back. His ears again caught the murmur of breathing that was almost a snore.

Rapidly and in silence he shoved into his overcoat and with body bent forward and head hanging, he went out.

THIRTY-FOUR

Three days later Vic called me again. His voice, half-raised, had stumbled back into the tense monotone. He had to see me today.

He came in.

Things were in a terrible mess, he said. He groaned and put his head down into his hands, burying the tears. He didn't know what to do. He hadn't phoned Loretta the next day but she had phoned him. The same urgency was in her as on the previous night. She had made up her mind to have him. She knew he loved her. This old-time business of honor was stupid. If he didn't do something decisive about it, she would. He had pleaded for her to wait in order for him to have time to work things out.

217

But she hadn't waited. She'd gone to see Cathy and she'd spilled things. And Cathy was furious. Cold and aloof in her now justifiable sense of having been offended.

He couldn't forgive Loretta for having done this. And Cathy wouldn't forgive him. She was keeping him out.

Cathy was bitter. "I can just see Vic giving Loretta what he never gives me. Spending time with her when he has no time for me. Talking to her when he won't talk to me. Loving her. Probably sleeping with her, though he says he hasn't . . ."

With me, Cathy was alternately cold and stormy. To Vic she was vindictively cold and hostile.

She became more depressed, feeling life had ended. "Except that I've got Ken. He's wonderful. He's been sweeter to me than he ever has been. As though he's sensed what's been going on."

And from Ken, who called and came in to see me: "I've been really afraid the last few days that Daddy might leave me with Mother. There's something all wrong.

"I keep wondering what it's all about. They still fight too much inside and not enough outwardly. Sometimes I think maybe they have financial worries and that's it. I know they have. But I think it's more the inside feelings that count.

"In the bedroom. That's where it's always the worst.

"They seem to be saying they wish it was all over with. They sit on the bed talking to each other. Maybe trying to love and having trouble. They've had too much trouble trying to love each other.

"I don't know what it is, but something happened. And I've been worried and scared that now they *will* break up the family and get a divorce. I'm mad at them for it. Why don't they grow up and get along? I'm mad at my father mostly for still not really trying to get at his feelings. He still pulls too much into himself, and that way he'll never get things straight.

"I don't like to think of their divorcing. It's frightening. Then I'd be my mother's only man."

For weeks Vic moved in a fog. And then something happened that, with its impact, brought long delayed decisiveness into his life.

It was a Saturday with the children home from school and Ken asked if he could go with his father to visit a job on which Vic was consulting.

Vic looked abstracted. "Why yes, Ken. Come on."

They went across the street together to where Vic had parked the car along the curb. Ken climbed in front in the seat next to Vic. Vic started the motor. And then it happened. With a racing engine Vic went crashing into the car parked ahead.

Ken was thrown forward against the windshield.

"I didn't know what had happened," Ken told me. "I only felt scared. I didn't know till afterward that I had a big lump on my forehead and cuts on my head and chin and fingers. I grabbed for the door and tried to open it. It was stuck someway, and that bothered me more than anything. I just had to get out and I finally did.

"I walked out and stood there and saw Mother coming across the street. And then I blacked out. When I came to, I was lying on the sidewalk. Daddy was walking away and Mother was still coming toward me. She came right to *me*. She didn't talk to Dad."

"I don't know how it happened," Vic said. "I don't see how it could have. The car parked in front of us was at least five

219

feet away. Even a poor driver could have maneuvered out easily. But I crashed into it. As if it were a premeditated act."

But this was not all. A few weeks later it happened again. Two accidents in such rapid succession!

"That coincidence," Ken muttered, "certainly had an awfully long arm."

He had stood the first accident with amazing fortitude, but this second one was too much for him. He came in wheezing, He felt that somehow the accidents had been his fault.

Why, I wondered, was he retreating to self-condemnation? For what was he punishing himself?

Soon I found out.

A few days before, Cathy had done an unusual thing. She had gone into the bathroom with Kenneth supposedly to help him into his pajamas. Quite incidentally, however, she had looked at his body in its eleven-year-old development.

"She looked at my hair there and told me I was growing big there. She told me I was growing into her man."

"So," I said, "you thought maybe that Daddy was trying to hurt you for that reason when he bumped the car. That he was jealous of your being Mother's man? And you're blaming yourself because in a way you'd like to be."

He assented and then retracted. "I did, I guess. But really it was all in *my* mind, not in Daddy's. I know my Daddy didn't mean to do it . . ."

For a moment I wondered whether to press truths that I knew he could grasp. But the horror and the terror of having to live with a father who wanted to harm him was too frightening as a certainty. Especially when he felt, as he'd said, that his father was not really working on his problems. Better to let it rest in the shadow of an imagined possibility from which Ken could choose to escape as he wished. Better to let him handle it by covering it over. For the present, at least. Of most importance for him now were his own feelings toward his father, rather than understanding his father's feelings toward him.

"How does the whole thing make you feel toward Daddy?" I asked.

He nodded knowingly and all at once the wheezing was cleared. "I guess that's one thing I've been hiding. I've been holding it in. He's so big. I've been kind of scared of saying it to myself. But I'm sore at him really. I'd like to do something violent to him. Maybe he didn't mean to do it. But I'm mad at him anyway. He should have been more careful. It *was* his fault. He had absolutely no excuse . . ."

As Ken went on angrily, he grew easier. He had not gotten at the ultimate reason for his anger. But he was at least placing his anger where he knew it belonged rather than turning it back onto himself.

To Vic, the impact of the whole episode kept growing. At first he tried to deny that unconscious motivations had played any role. Then something came out that helped him. One part of the first accident had bothered him more than any other. This stuck in his mind until one night, in the group therapy session, he confronted Cathy with it.

"*I* was in that accident, too, Cathy. I, too, was in the smash. It wasn't only Ken who was in the car. I was there when it hit. But you . . . how did you act? As if there were no one there but Kenneth. You came across the street, Cathy, and you didn't say one word to me. You passed me by and went straight to Ken . . ."

Cathy and Ken! Ken and Cathy! The combination made a pattern in his mind which met with another pattern. His own pattern long ago.

221

For days and nights the tremendous import of this filled him until from out of the crucible of the deep suffering in him there rose a conviction stronger than words.

At last Vic knew that he couldn't let this happen to his son, the thing that had happened to him. His father had left home. His father had left him with his mother. He himself had been leaving home virtually, seldom being there and when he was there not really being present. Being abstracted and away, his feelings apart. He was leaving Ken with Cathy as his father had left him with his mother.

He couldn't let this thing happen. He had to dig in and stop escaping.

Vic knew finally that he had to become a man.

THIRTY-FIVE

Many months later Vic brought into another group therapy session something that had happened to him the previous night.

It seemed that the white moon had been shining in the window onto Cathy as she lay asleep beside him in bed. He had raised himself on his elbow and had looked down on her to see if she was all right, since she had just recovered from a rather heavy cold. A sense of eeriness crept into him as he watched the covers rise and fall with her breathing. Her face was relaxed, her lips slightly parted. From between them came the slightest of snores.

He caught his breath, his chest tightening, the dryness coming into his mouth. Panic filled him. He wanted to run. To get up and get out.

This had happened before. With Loretta. But earlier also. With his mother when he was a boy. The rise and fall of her body as she breathed. Her closeness in bed. The small snore creeping out with its rhythmic hum.

How many had been the times when he had been filled with ineffable yearning to reach out and run his hand through her long, soft hair. Being with his mother was good and close and warm. Until his father came home.

Vic had told himself that his mother preferred him to his father. That when his father returned home and he, Vic, was shoved off into the small room across the hall, his mother's mood would slip from its ordinary unsmiling and serious quiet into sadness that held in it the quality of resignation.

And then Vic recalled an incident he'd lost long ago.

His father had come home on the previous night and Vic once more had been put to bed in his own room. The next day he got up before the pale morning moon was out of the sky. He'd dressed himself quietly, somehow vaguely planning to go outside in search of something. Something perhaps to fill the lonely void inside him.

He opened and closed his bedroom door and stood in the hall, the door to his mother's room darkly closed. And then it was that the sounds came to him which for all the years since he had been struggling to keep lost. Little chirruping unwonted sounds creeping out through his mother's closed door. And the sound of her laughter, secretively gay.

This quiet woman who, he'd always believed, was sexless. This serious woman who never laughed! His father was doing something to her to make her lips part in this gurgling enjoyment.

After his father had gone again and Vic was back once more in his mother's bed, night after night he would rise on his elbow and gaze at his mother sleeping.

Then the wish would creep into him along with the shadowed fear that made him slice off the wish before it pushed over the threshhold into awareness—the wish to know what secret things he, too, might do to her to make her laugh.

Long after the episode lay buried, the wishes still prompted him to run away. He left home as soon as he was old enough to get a job. He travelled across many states to remove himself physically from that which he carried with him, ironically, in his innermost thoughts.

"I see it now," Vic said, a new composure showing in the increased easiness and strength in his voice. "Some of you people in this group take refuge in confusion. My way has been to take refuge in composure. My calm, cool quietness was a way of escaping the thoughts and feelings I felt I had to escape . . ."

He glanced at the doctor, smiling in sudden hesitance and letting his eyes drop, still somewhat fearful that this man whom he now took as a kind of father might punish him as his real father might have if he'd seen into his thoughts. The doctor might perhaps reach out and burn a hole into him with his cigarette, as his real father might have burned a far graver, deeper wound with a branding iron. Like the hole in the figurine on his mother's ivory brush. Like a hole his father might have slashed with his keen-edged razor.

"I can see now," Vic continued, "that any reaction I have had to any woman is essentially a reaction to my mother. I took refuge in the composed assurance that I'd solved my problem by leaving it when I left home. But I hadn't. I hadn't left my mother. She was still with me, inside me. I carried her across the country with me. And I carried along with her all my reactions of fear about getting close to a woman. Cathy! Loretta! It wouldn't have mattered who.

"But now that that's out in the open, I don't need to run after some Loretta-shaped promise to happiness. I can see that it's up to me to clear out the underbrush, and then the road to happiness with Cathy won't be too hard. She's really the woman I want."

Gradually as the months passed Cathy, too, saw things. One night in the group something was said that made her slip back into what she had used as *her* refuge, the sweet, martyred, long-suffering air behind which she hid the feelings that made her afraid.

This touched off something in another group member, a man who was full of the fury he had carried from his past. He sprang up now and took it out on Cathy. "You're just like my mother," he shouted, "with your holier-than-thou attitude."

He rose and started across the room toward her, towering in his violence, his fists whitely clenched.

For a split second, Cathy's teeth flashed in white and gleaming exultation and the flush of excitement flooded into her cheeks. Then she flinched and paled and started trembling. She wanted to run, but she stayed.

She was frightened by violence and excited by violence, both. She veered from violence and steered toward violence, both. The happiest days of her life had been when her father had turned to her. And this he had done in violence more than in peace. Her only sure way of getting her father had been to provoke him to the point of violence. Then in the mad bursting of temper he became all hers.

"His spankings were the only way through which I could consistently get him."

His spankings actually had been his most dependable gift.

But violence could become too violent and hurt could become too grave. The fear had grown to overshadow the excitement, and Cathy had sought safety in marrying a man unlike her father, mild and retiring, with whom she could control her own feelings along with the control she exerted over him.

That she had needed also to control Blaine she came to see far more clearly, and why. She had wanted a man, yes. But only a man whom she could dominate. Otherwise, in her own excitement, she might provoke hurt beyond endurance, such as her father might have given her a long, long time since.

Gradually Cathy saw these things in their many-sided aspects with the shadows and the colors reaching from them. As she was able to show these to her doctor-father and her therapist-mother without being destroyed as she had feared in her childhood that her own father and mother might destroy her, she grew less fearful. She no longer needed to take refuge in tenseness and apologetic sweetness. Moreover, she could let her most impelling wish come to flower—her deep and basic wish to have a man.

Time moved on. Changes came into being slowly—almost imperceptibly. Like the shift of the seasons. Barely noticeable, the changing, till the change was there.

Vic was Cathy's man now. And she was his woman. There were fights between them as there always would be and always are in a marriage that has any vigor. But there were moments of ecstasy also, and moments of peace.

THIRTY-SIX

Several months later Cathy told me of an episode that she thought might make Ken feel he needed me. It had happened on Sunday afternoon. Vic had brought home some work and had it spread out on the dining room table. Cathy was doing the family mending and Ken and Brad, Gene and some other neighbor children were playing kick-ball in the front yard with a new basketball that Kenneth had recently gotten. All of a sudden she heard a loud explosion. Then a medley of angry voices and screams from Brad. Dashing to the window she and Vic saw that Kenneth's ball had been run over by a passing car and Ken was beating Brad with great fury.

The next minute, Brad came dashing into the room, howling, Kenneth on Brad's heels, still belaboring him, hammering at him with both fists.

"Brad kicked my ball on purpose," he yelled. "He kicked it right in front of the car." Brad shrieked that he hadn't. But a sly grin slipped across his face.

Vic stepped in positively and had the boys sit down, Cathy and he with them.

"Now," said Cathy, "let's take turns and each tell what happened. Kenneth, want to go first?"

"Well," said Ken, "Brad held the ball toward the street, like this, and when the car got close he kicked it out onto the street so it would go right in front of the car."

Brad protested, "I did not. It was an accident."

"Well, then," challenged Ken, "why did you grin like this when you saw the car was going to hit the ball?" He made an ugly leer in his attempt to imitate Brad. "You did it deliberately. You . . . you . . ."

"Both of you are very angry," Cathy commented, "Ken at Brad and Brad at Ken. I know Ken's mad about the ball and Brad is probably mad about other things. Mad feelings are better out than in, and talking them out is a better way than slugging them out, so let's go. Right here."

Both boys jumped in. Brad was mad that Ken had refused to read the comics to him. Ken was mad that Brad had awakened him at five-thirty to read them. Each went on with his own private string of grievances.

"What would you like to do to each other?" Vic asked after a while.

"I'd like to hit him and hit him for about an hour!" Ken decided.

"And I'd like to too!" added Brad.

But the anger was on the wane.

"O.K.," Vic concluded. "I guess that's about it." Then, with an attempt to end on a light note, he added, "When the ball got hit it surely made a good loud pop. I thought it was a blow-out at first. It really banged!"

Without a word, Kenneth was up and across the room. His face contorted in fury, he dived at Vic and began to hammer at him.

Vic warded him off. "Hey, wait a minute. Sit down, Ken. Let's talk about this."

Reluctantly Kenneth went back to his chair, his face red with rage, the angry tears streaking down his cheeks.

"What made you so mad at me, Ken?" Vic's voice held no rancor but a real desire to understand.

"You were making fun of my ball getting ruined. And I don't think it was funny!" from Ken.

"But I didn't mean to make fun of you, Ken. I'm sorry. Maybe . . . maybe . . . the ball getting run over was like you getting hurt. Was that it?"

"Yes. It was like my legs or something getting hurt. It wasn't funny."

"Or maybe something even more important getting hurt?"

Ken nodded and hung his head.

"Yes, I know, Ken. Sometimes a boy's kick-ball or anything that belongs to him seems almost like a part of him. I apologize for saying what I did; I just didn't think. I'm really sorry."

Ken smiled shyly across at Vic. "That's O.K., I guess."

"And," said Vic, "Of course we'll get you another ball."

That had been all for the moment. But Cathy felt that Kenneth was still brooding.

"Let's see what happens," I said.

"Maybe he'll call."

A week later he did.

When he came in he told me of the episode. "But," he said,

"that's only a minor part of the whole. This week has been my bad luck week. Everything seems to have gone wrong. I lost my bus book with twenty-five tickets in it. Brad's been so irritating I've had a hard time not socking him. And to pile on the hurt, Hamburger grabbed my jelly doughnut right out of my hand and ate it. But worst, I got failures in spelling and in handwriting, and my free-hand drawing isn't good. And to make even more disaster, I sprained my thumb."

"What a lot of things going wrong with your hand," I observed. "You let the ticket book and the jelly doughnut slip out of your hand, so to speak. You have to keep your hand from socking Brad. And spelling and writing and drawing are all things you do with your hand. And you have to hurt it, to cap the climax. What on earth are you punishing it for?"

"I know what you mean," he grinned. "But I don't do much of that any more."

"Since when?"

He tried to place it. The clues that he gave took me back to the accidents, and it occurred to me that all the things about which he was complaining might be residuals dating from them and carrying with them the dregs of things much further back. The recent episode of the kick-ball had set them off.

As old tea leaves left in a tea cup color fresh water that is poured in, so can feelings that are left as residue color what comes in with fresh experience. So, no doubt, had Ken's feelings left from the accidents continued to color what had come to him since.

Vic had changed. By now he had moved into a place of greater security with Cathy. His unconsciously motivated impulse to hurt Ken was gone. But the residue of old feelings which Ken carried in him could keep Ken from accepting Vic's new fatherliness toward him. However, if Kenneth could now face what he had chosen at the time of the accidents to bury, he might be able to lay the ghosts with reassurance that the danger lay in the past and was now no more threatening than is anything else that is dead and gone. Then he would be better able to develop the sturdy sort of relationship with his father that every child needs.

Presently Ken went on to tell me of a dream, and the dream made me certain that connecting what he was now feeling with the accidents had been right. And Vic's jesting remark about the basketball had added fuel to the fire.

In the dream Kenneth was surrounded by enemy forces. There were ground forces and a tank and a great plane flying over. The ground forces had faces strangely like Brad's. "But they're not too dangerous really. If they were alone I could manage them quite well, I think.

"As for the tank, it rumbled and roared." He laughed with the thought that linked itself to this. "That's the way Mother's been—a rumbling, roaring woman. In the dream she was coming toward me, roaring down on me, rumbling down. I had to get out of the way quick, and I did. Otherwise she might have rolled over me. Then she would have squashed me and I wouldn't have been able to breathe, not with a tank strangling my chest. It would have felt the way it was when I used to have asthma."

But the gravest danger lay from the plane overhead. It might inflict even more gruesome injury and destruction than the tank ever could have. . . . "Like some bigger force behind all the rest and it could hurt me more . . ."

"More than crushing your chest?"

"Oh yes, much more, Dorothy. He would shoot me, shoot my leg off . . ."

I thought of those first days with Ken! Of his wounded soldier. And I listened carefully as he went on. "Only it wouldn't be only my leg. It might be my penis, too, because he didn't like its giving me pleasure . . ."

"Like when?"

He was hesitant and his eyes closed as if he were trying with great effort to drag something out that was hard to remember. And then it came, softly, almost in a whisper, "Like when mother touched me. No, she didn't, though . . ." He looked puzzled. "Why did I say she touched me? She didn't, but I thought she had . . ."

"Or you sort of hoped she might when she looked at you and told you that you were getting big there?"

He opened his eyes and smiled. "Yes, Dorothy. How on earth did you know?"

We talked, then, of how he had been keeping his hands from doing many things as well as keeping them from giving him the feelings that recalled this scene with his mother in the bathroom so fraught with danger. And we agreed that a month later he would come to tell me how he was progressing.

He came in, glad. "I've gotten all A's in my spelling and writing since I saw you. And my drawing is much better. Oh boy! Were you right about my hand!"

We talked again about his father and the accident several times at wide intervals of months. Much simmering went on in his mind in between. And the thing finally came clear and straight. He could comprehend without anguish that unconscious feelings had pressed his father into trying to hurt him because his father had been jealous of his position with his mother.

This had revived many earlier fears that his father might hurt him for his having wanted to be the "onliest" with his

233

mother—fears that he had often expressed in his play. A.
when he'd recoiled over the red paint and had brought ou
thoughts of father and of being cut. Or again as when he had
pictured himself as a mean little plane momentarily success
ful in rivalling his father only to be destroyed by the father
plane flying near. In other words, the accidents were like evi
dence that the earlier fears had been true.

"In his unconscious mind at the time of the accidents
Daddy wanted to hurt me. Disagreeable as this sounds, I can
see now that it was only natural. I was in strong with Mother
The accidents were when he was weak with her. He probably
felt that if he eliminated me he might get in stronger. That
was his opportunity. He was sort of trying to get even with me
for stealing Mother."

He smiled suddenly a bit sheepishly: "That's the way I
used to want to do to him!"

"Like you showed me in those battles you used to play?"

"Yes," he assented and returned to more recent days.

"In his conscious mind I don't think my father wants to
hurt me, but his unconscious mind was making him so jittery
he didn't know what he was doing. The accidents happened
because he wasn't working straight on his angriness. So it had
to come out in roundabout ways. It led him into those things
he couldn't help, like my unconscious used to lead me into the
asthma.

"And as for me, instead of my staying good and mad at
Daddy because he bumped me, I was scared and let my anger
sneak out onto Brad.

"Now that I think of it, I guess I was mad at Daddy for
something else, too. He got me out of being the onliest one
with my mother after I'd waited so long to get there. In one

234

way it's been hard, having him deprive me of some of Mother's love. In another way, it's been better.

"Either no love to a boy or all the mother's love to a boy sure messes things up for him. First it was one way for me; then it was the other.

"Now it's more even. Daddy takes his position more and I don't have quite so many privileges and compliments. But the gains outweigh the losses. Since Daddy takes his position better, I'm not so burdened. It's as if he felt bigger. I think he must be getting out what was bothering him inside. It shows. Why, in his disagreements with Mother now, he sticks to his point rather than being an in-between man. His contribution to their conversation used to be wavering and practically nil. He'd dodge around. But now he says what he really means.

"And as for my mother, you say all boys sort of dream of having their mothers for their wives till they hitch up with girl friends. Well, I do still sometimes. But she doesn't take me as her guardian angel any more, so it's more just in my mind, which gives me more control over it.

"She goes much more for Daddy. I think they must have their bedroom troubles ironed out. They're happier there, and that's where it counts. I'm glad."

He paused a moment, sat up, smiling at me. "Yes," he repeated, "and I'm glad for another reason also. It would have been awful, you see, if Mother had stayed dependent on me. I would have *had* to disappoint her. I couldn't have kept it to her-and-me for too much longer. Because now that I'm in Junior High School where the girls are real, real pretty, I'll be getting to have girl-friends soon. I feel it coming. It won't be long now. I'm growing up."

Kenneth had spent two and a half years coming to me regularly. Three years had passed since then, during which he had asked to see me occasionally as he had felt the need. Perhaps he would come again. Perhaps he would not.

If life grew too hard or too heavy, he might always retreat into asthma. That had been the pattern laid down by the fact that his constitution had furnished him with this potential for refuge and escape. But because of the understanding he had of himself and of his own feelings, it would take a lot more now to throw him. He no longer needed to flee from feelings he had formerly blocked because they made him too guilty and anxious. He could bring these out now into the open rather than escape into asthmatic attacks. This he had shown.

Meanwhile, as Ken said, he was growing up. As he left my office that day, I watched him go through the door. He was shooting up, tall like his father, bright and limber, his hair bright gold.

Not every small boy or girl can spend over two years in a psychotherapist's office. I wondered when we would know better how to help children more widely in schools and homes to understand their feelings, and when we would be able to help parents understand theirs, so that the boys and girls now growing up might know not only about tanks and bullets but about the most powerful of all weapons for both good and evil—the human feelings that propel us, if we do not understand them, into hating in place of loving, into killing instead of creation.

I looked ahead and saw in Kenneth the possibility of a new generation—the hope of a new world.

To you who are parents:

As you've read about Kenneth and his parents, perhaps you have wondered: "What does all of this have to do with my child and me? Surely my child has never had the kind of thoughts and feelings Ken had!" Or, if your child is still very small, "Surely he never will have them."

Convinced as you may be, this is not true.

ALL CHILDREN HAVE THE SAME KIND OF THOUGHTS AND FEELINGS THAT KENNETH HAD.

All normal children are interested in their bodies and in their body-feelings. Watch a baby. See how he likes to be petted and stroked, how he likes to suck; the pleasure it gives him. Even at this age, before thoughts form, the body-feelings are present.

As he grows, he becomes interested in bowel movements and finds body-pleasure in elimination. You can read it in the self-satisfied expression on his face if you watch in an unprejudiced way when he is quite small. As he develops in his thinking, he makes up fantasies about these things which are so intimate to him, so near at hand and so close. This is natural.

As he advances, he wonders more about his body and its functions. All children do. They wonder not only about their own bodies but about the bodies of others, and are more or less concerned with similarities and differences between the sexes and between grown-ups and themselves. All children are interested in hollows and protuberances and connect these up in conscious or unconscious fantasies with maleness and femaleness. All children are interested in impregnation,

237

gestation and birth and imagine all kinds of things about sex and love. To a lesser or greater degree all little girls wonder if they may perhaps have lost that appendage that seems to be most highly prized and all little boys worry for fear they may lose theirs; all little girls make up stories about getting rid of mother and marrying father and all little boys make up stories about getting rid of father and marrying mother. These things are a normal part of growing up. They are not signs of problems but of normal development. The fantasies that accompany them are normal too. In essence they resemble Kenneth's fantasies, though each individual child adds touches and colors of his own.

Because rivalry with a big person enters into the fantasies of being husband to mother or wife to father, a certain amount of fear also enters and of guilt. Threats and insinuations as to what might happen if children masturbate may contribute further anxiety and guilt. In consequence, our children repress their fantasies as they continue growing. They drop them down into the hamper of the unconscious and if we ask, "Did you ever think such thoughts?" they look at us blankly and say, "Of course, *no*."

The same thing has happened to us. As we were growing, we ourselves had similar thoughts even though we, too, may declare, "I never had them." These thoughts or fantasies still lie in our unconscious minds and in some way still affect us in our present-day living. If it were not for a boy's early fantasies about loving his mother, he would make a far less tender husband. The propulsion of these fantasies into the present may affect us for good or evil, positively or negatively. Fantasies about love and sex and body-feelings become negative only as they are invested too heavily with guilt and anxiety and resentment.

238

Fantasies may also show up in the personality far removed from where they started, their beginnings completely disguised. The little boy, for instance, who held in his bowel movements in order to annoy and punish his mother may become the man who holds onto his money and is stingy with his wife and family. The little girl who began making up fantasies about having lost her precious protuberance may grow into the woman who tries to compensate in her marriage by wearing the pants. In the shyness that disturbs us when seeking intimacy it is not difficult to recognize that direct connections with lost fantasies may exist. It is more difficult to see, when shyness causes us to be inept in business or in broader social contacts, that this may go back just as truly to fear and guilt which accumulated around forgotten childhood thoughts similar to Ken's.

All normal children have angry and resentful feelings which at times lead to fantasies of wanting to kill.

Many parents have become aware of this and know how to help children channel such feelings into harmless activities.* Ordinarily the anger and resentment seep out in naughtiness of one sort or another. But some children, like Kenneth, have shut such hostility in too hard and are "too good." We can be fairly sure, then, that at least two things have happened. First, the hostility having accumulated without normal outlets will be over-abundant. Second, it will be over-heavily laden with fear and with guilt.

It is here, if anywhere, that Kenneth might be termed "not normal." He had an over-abundance of hostility stored in-

---

* See for instance *New Ways in Discipline*, in which I have discussed what a good many parents are thinking and doing about this sort of thing.

side him, having blocked it excessively, and he had it far too heavily over-loaded with anxiety and with guilt.

Kenneth's hostility was in essence, however, no different from any other child's. It was simply *bigger*. The blocking off or repression of it was bigger. The anxiety and guilt were bigger. And these feelings, in turn, invaded other areas of Kenneth's feeling life. He carried a heavier load of hostility over into the sexual area than do many children; making bigger "clubs" and dreaming dreams somewhat more violent than the violence that is present in every normal male's primitive cave-man wish to attack. Ken carried a heavier load of anxiety and guilt into almost everything he did, not even daring to show his aggression in a normal attack on school subjects.

But, to reiterate, the *kind* of feelings Kenneth had were normal. They were not essentially different from those in all children. Some of them were merely enlarged.

When a small snapshot is blown up, everything on it stands out more clearly. A darn on the shirt that went unnoticed now shows its criss-cross stitching. A scar on the cheek emerges which has not shown in the smaller picture. Just so in the portrait of Kenneth, resentment and anxiety and guilt that in many children go unnoticed stand out in clear evidence, not because they are different but because they are *bigger*.

This had happened because in the beginning Kenneth had had neither his mother nor his father to trust.

Now to the crux of what all of this has to do with you, the parent. *What you feel is more important than what you say or do.* Often children get your feelings no matter how much you try to hide them. They react to your feelings more

240

than to your words or to any external techniques you may use in their upbringing.

Doctors have observed in hospital nurseries that even newborn infants respond to feelings. A nurse who doesn't really like babies gets more crying in her hours of duty than the nurse who gives love as well as care.

Nonetheless, as children grow, they do sometimes misinterpret what their parents do for them. They misinterpret their parents' care and good intentions. Their fantasies are colored then by these misinterpretations, and their resentments and anxieties and guilt mount to proportions which produce problems. The more firmly we provide a framework of love and understanding in the lives of our children, the more securely are they able to navigate through childhood's bizarre fantasies and to move on to a more realistic footing with things-as-they-are.

If we can become truly aware that all children do have these fantasies, this, of itself, will increase our understanding. If we can accept fantasies such as Kenneth's as a natural and normal part of our own children's childhood, this will make us feel with them in new ways which they are bound to sense.

You have encountered Kenneth's thoughts and feelings throughout these pages. If you can now come to understand that they are not unique in Kenneth nor abnormal, this understanding will communicate itself to your child.

Perhaps, then, because of your new inner feeling, your child will bring out some of his thoughts about love and life, about bodies and sex; some of his strange wishes and fears, or at least some of those which are still in his conscious mind. Perhaps he will; perhaps he will not. You needn't try to induce him to. And you definitely won't probe for what may lie beneath the threshold of consciousness. You aren't a trained psychotherapist. But, being attuned, you may hear things you have never heard before, you may notice things you have never noticed. And, being attuned, you will be able to take with greater equanimity whatever he brings. Moreover, you will be able to sense better if he seems too tense or anxious. And you will know that such tensions may have their roots in his fantasies rather than in any specific things you've done or not done.

You'll know, too, that getting help from a clinic or therapist is a friendly process, not a terrifying ordeal. You will know that just as adults are helped by talking out their feelings, so children are helped by playing out theirs. Having watched Ken move through his play-therapy, you will know what is meant by play-therapy.

Above all, you will know that even though your children may never talk about their fantasies, they still have them. Either in the present or the past they, too, have had the same kinds of thoughts and feelings as Ken had. Your possessing this knowledge may not consciously change your actions. But insofar as it changes your feelings into warmer and more loving understanding, so also will it change the atmosphere in which your children carry on their growing up.

It is never late to have this kind of change come into being. Whenever it comes, it brings with it an increase in ease and confidence which makes us better friends with our children and so better parents in the deepest and most strengthening sense.